THE FIGHT FOR SURVIVAL

The warrior rose to hurl a lance.

Nate had no boulders to duck behind. Nor could he retreat. He was too exposed. So he did the last thing the warrior expected. Nate threw himself at him, drawing his Bowie as he sprang.

The warrior let fly. The lance was a blur, cleaving the air like wooden lightning. Only the fact that the warrior's horse was skittishly prancing saved Nate's life. The lance passed over Nate's shoulder, and then he was close enough to sink the Bowie into the warrior's thigh.

Howling in rage and pain, the Ute drew his own knife and launched himself at Nate. Nate was bigger but the impact bowled him over. He seized the Ute's knife arm as they fell. Locked together, they rolled side to side, each seeking to gain an advantage.

Nate heard Chases Rabbits yell something. Suddenly the ground seemed to give way. The Ute looked up in surprise. Belatedly, Nate divined what had happened. In their thrashing, they had rolled over the edge and were tumbling down the talus....

The *Wilderness* series:

#46
WILDERNESS
UNTAMED COUNTRY

David Thompson

LEISURE BOOKS NEW YORK CITY

Dedicated to Judy, Joshua and Shane.

A LEISURE BOOK®

August 2005

Published by

Dorchester Publishing Co., Inc.
200 Madison Avenue
New York, NY 10016

ISBN 0-8439-5459-0

The name "Leisure Books" and the stylized "L" with design are trademarks of Dorchester Publishing Co., Inc.

Printed in the United States of America.

Visit us on the web at www.dorchesterpub.com.

UNTAMED COUNTRY

Chapter One

There were eight of them, riding in single file. They did not spot the lurker in the trees.

Nate King was in the lead, astride a dust-caked bay. A big man with night-black hair and piercing green eyes, he had once been a free trapper. That was back in the days when beaver pelts fetched prime prices, before silk hats came along and knocked the stuffing out of the beaver market. Now he called himself a mountaineer. He and his family lived where few whites dared, in the untamed country more commonly known as the Rocky Mountains.

Like two other men in his party, Nate wore buckskins and had an ammo pouch and possibles bag slanted across his broad chest. A brace of pistols adorned his waist. Cradled in the crook of his left elbow was a new Hawken rifle he recently bought in St. Louis.

Behind Nate came his wife, Winona, a full-bodied Shoshone whose beauty was such that it turned white and red heads alike. Her beaded doeskin dress was a testament to the home arts she had mastered at an early age. Winona was tired, but she rode with her head high and her back straight. She was a proud woman, Winona King, and she would not show weakness in front of her man.

Behind Winona came her daughter, Evelyn. In her early teens, Evelyn was on the cusp of the magical transformation from girl into woman. Her eyes had a thoughtfulness about them rare for one of her tender years, and on her pretty face was the stamp of hardships few girls her age ever experienced.

After Evelyn came her older brother, Zach. A firebrand, he resented it when anyone referred to him as a half-breed. Yet his fiery temper was one of the traits for which those who shared his accident of birth were most noted.

Close behind Zach rode Louisa, his wife. Petite yet sturdy, she wore her hair in a mannish cut, and buckskin britches instead of a dress. She yawned as they neared the crest of a final ridge, then glanced back and grinned at the oldster whose white mare plodded along behind her sorrel. "It won't be much longer, Shakespeare."

Shakespeare McNair grunted. His hair and beard were as white as the vestiges of snow that capped some of the surrounding peaks, his features as craggy as nearby cliffs. Of all the mountain men, he had lived in the wilds the longest. A legend among his kind, it was often joked that he was as old as

Methuselah, which was only a little shy of the truth.

To the woman behind him, whose hair was streaked with gray but whose face and figure were those a younger woman would envy, Shakespeare was more than a legend. He was her husband. Her mate. Her man. And Blue Water Woman loved him with a passion as boundless as the sea of grass they had crossed to reach the Rockies.

Bringing up the rear was a giant warrior. Touch the Clouds wore leggings and moccasins and held a lance in his right hand. A quiver and a bow were strung across his back, and a long knife hung on his left hip. A leader of the Shoshones, he was renowned as much for his devotion to the welfare of his people as for his prowess in battle.

These, then, were the eight dusty travelers returning to the land they loved from that which men called civilization. They had endured much. All had nearly lost their lives on one occasion or another. They were eager to be home. So eager that in their fatigue and their anticipation they forgot the most important lesson the wilderness had to impart: They must never, ever let down their guard.

Nate King was reaching up to rub the stubble on his square chin when a gleam of light in a stand of pines above and to his left caught his attention. It was the sort of flash made by the reflection of sunlight on metal. He had seen this kind of gleam before, and while there might be a perfectly innocent explanation, it had been Nate's experience that those who lived the longest on the frontier were those who realized danger came in many guises and shapes.

So superbly honed were Nate's reflexes that a heartbeat after he saw the flash, he reined his bay to the right and bawled to the others, "Take cover!"

A rifle shot cracked, unnaturally loud in the rarefied mountain air. Nate thought he heard the buzz of lead past his head, and then he ducked low and rode hellbent for cover. He heard his daughter-in-law cry out.

"Zach! No!"

Nate twisted in the saddle. His son was barreling up the slope toward the pines, whooping at the top of his lungs. It was rash, foolhardy, gloriously brave. Without hesitation, Nate reined after him and jabbed his heels against the bay.

"Damned kids!" Shakespeare McNair fumed. "They have not so much brains as ear wax!" Yet despite that, he charged after them.

The three women and the girl looked at one another. Their expressions betrayed their thoughts. They thought their men were reckless. They thought it wiser to seek cover. But the next moment they were in full gallop up the slope, for if there was one trait of which the King family and Blue Water Woman could never be accused, it was cowardice. They would give their lives for their families, as they had proven time and again.

Zach King spied rising tendrils of gun smoke and veered toward them. He gave voice to another war whoop. Someone had tried to kill his father, and that someone would pay. Fierce exultation coursed through his veins as he saw a shadowy figure rise from concealment. But the exultation changed to consternation when he saw the figure shove a ramrod into a rifle. The would-be assassin had reloaded faster than he anticipated.

Nate King saw the figure, too. An icy hand seized his heart as the bushwhacker whipped the rifle to a shoulder to fire at his son. Instinctively, Nate snapped his Hawken to his own shoulder and fired, knowing full well that to hit a target from a full gallop took as much luck as skill. He was sure he missed. But he was just as sure that his shot came close enough to cause the lurker in the trees to whirl and bolt.

Zach reined to the left to reach the would-be assassin that much sooner. In his haste and his excitement, he failed to pay attention to the trees he was plunging into. As a result, a low limb materialized before him as if out of nowhere, and before he could duck, the limb caught him across the chest and lifted him clean off his horse.

Shakespeare McNair grinned. "Kids!" he again declared. He slowed, though, and shouted to Zach as he came abreast, "Are you all right?" The younger King, clutching his chest and swearing luridly, his face the color of a turnip, nodded and waved Shakespeare on.

The figure in the trees came to a bareback pinto and vaulted onto it without breaking stride. A slap of his legs and the pinto was off, bounding with the speed of a rabbit being chased by coyotes.

Nate was close enough to use a pistol, but he didn't draw one. If at all possible, he wanted to take the shooter alive—or, at the very least, alive enough to say why the man tried to kill them.

Nate had his share of enemies. Anyone who lived in the mountains for any length of time was bound to run into hostile Indians or renegade whites, and the enemies who lived to ride away inevitably showed up another day. Nate could think of half a dozen warriors from half a dozen tribes who would give their best warhorse to have his hair hanging in their lodge. Maybe this was one of them. The shooter was definitely an Indian. The long raven braids, the swarthy, muscular form, the breech-clout and moccasins left no doubt. But which tribe? Nate wondered.

To many whites east of the Mississippi River, all Indians looked pretty much the same. A statement Nate heard voiced time and again. But to someone like him, who had lived among Indians, no two tribes were alike. Their manner of dress, the way they wore their hair, their bodies, their features, combined to identify which tribe a warrior was from just as the same traits identified an Irishman or a Frenchman from a Spaniard.

Now, as the pinto burst from shadows into the sunlight, Nate had his first good look. To say he was surprised was to phrase it mildly.

The warrior was a Ute. A young Ute, all lean sinew and bone. Yet Nate was on peaceful terms with the Utes and had been for years, ever since he helped parley a truce between the Utes and the

Shoshones. Not that long ago, he had helped a Ute band rid themselves of a vicious grizzly, and their chief had professed undying friendship from that day on.

Why, then, was this young Ute warrior out for their blood? Nate brought the bay to a full gallop, heedless of the heightened risk. He needed answers, and he would have them, come Hell or Armageddon.

Shakespeare McNair was also puzzled. He had seen the Ute, and could not fathom the stripling's motive. The Utes were not as bloodthirsty as, say, the Sioux or the Blackfeet. They did not hate whites on general principle, although Shakespeare was of the opinion that their feelings would change as more and more white men came to the Rockies. Whites now laid claim to all the land between the Atlantic and the Mississippi, and it wouldn't be long before they were bursting at the seams and eager to acquire the other half of the continent.

Shakespeare dreaded that day. He loved the mountains. He cherished his freedom and his privacy. Civilization would change things, would bring with it the man-made laws and rules that caged a man as surely as iron bars. He saw no difference between civilization and chains, and he hated shackles of any kind.

A shot snapped McNair out of his reflection. The young Ute had tried again to shoot at Nate King.

Nate had hunched low over his saddle when the warrior turned, but the slug came nowhere near him. On he raced, narrowing the distance. The Ute had slowed when he fired, a mistake that would shortly cost him.

Gripping the Hawken by the barrel, Nate bore down on his quarry. He had a clear shot at the Ute, but he did not take it. His arm poised, he focused on the Ute to the exclusion of all else.

A hint of panic marked the young warrior's next glance. He was goading his pinto for all he was worth, but the pinto was no match for Nate's bay. The pinto was fleet, but it lacked stamina, and in the mountains the ability to outlast an adversary counted for more than being the fastest.

Twenty yards separated them, then ten yards, then five. Nate felt a twinge in his side from a bear attack not long ago, but he ignored it. Raising the Hawken higher, he leaned to his right. Within moments, the bay was neck and neck with the pinto.

The Ute did what any cornered wolf would do. He lashed out, swinging his rifle at Nate's face. But Nate was quicker; he slammed his Hawken into the young warrior's shoulder.

A yelp, and the Ute tumbled. He hit hard on his shoulder and lost his grip on his rifle. Rolling up into a crouch, he drew a long-bladed knife. He had to be hurting, but he did not show it.

. Nate drew rein so roughly, the bay slewed to a stop, churning clods of dirt. Reining around, Nate let go of the reins and grabbed a pistol. "Drop it!" he commanded in the Ute tongue. He was not as fluent in Ute as he was in Shoshone, but he knew enough to get by.

The young warrior did no such thing. Incredibly,

although Nate's pistol was trained on his torso, he hurled himself at the bay. Nate thought the Ute meant to spring at him, but instead the young warrior man slashed at the bay's forelegs.

Until that moment, Nate had kept a level head. He wasn't mad that the Ute tried to kill him. It wasn't as if this were the first time something like this happened. Deadly occurrences were part and perilous parcel of life in the wilderness. But shooting at him was one thing, trying to cripple his horse another. With a low oath, Nate hurled himself from the saddle.

The Ute tried to skip back out of reach, but he wasn't quite quick enough. Nate swung the Hawken and caught the young warrior on the shoulder, spinning him half around.

In midair, Nate twisted so he alighted on his feet like a cat. He was set to swing again, but the Ute was not inclined to trade blows.

The young warrior fled.

Nate gave instant chase. He was considered swift, but it was soon apparent the younger man had an edge. Try as he might, he couldn't catch up. Quite the contrary. The Ute was slowly pulling ahead.

All Nate had to do was point his pistol and fire, but he couldn't bring himself to shoot the Ute in the back. So on he ran, pacing himself so he would last longer. The youth glanced over a shoulder and his dark eyes widened.

Nate thought it was because of him. Then hooves pounded, and Shakespeare McNair swept past on the white mare. "Don't kill him!" Nate shouted.

Shakespeare wasn't planning to. He wanted answers as much as Nate. Waiting until he was almost on top of his panicked quarry, Shakespeare shot him high in the right shoulder. The impact flung the youth to the ground as if he had been punched by a giant fist.

Nate stood over the sprawled form and thumbed back the hammer of his pistol. At the distinct *click* the young Ute glanced up, then slowly rolled over, his teeth gritted against the pain. He was bleeding, but not badly. Judging by the entry and exit wounds, Nate could tell the slug had spared the collarbone. McNair had placed the shot well.

The young warrior moved his fingers in sign language. "You shot me, old man!" He seemed surprised.

Shakespeare was at Nate's elbow. "I will shoot you again," he signed, "if you do not do as I tell you."

"Shoot me," the youth signed. "I will gladly die."

Shakespeare sighed and shook his head, then said in English to Nate, "What an arrogant, rascally, beggarly, lousy knave it is."

"More William S.?" Nate asked, referring to the famed Bard of Avon. McNair could quote his namesake by the hour.

"Who else?" Shakespeare turned back to the Ute. "Why did you try to kill my friend?"

"Grizzly Killer must die," the youth signed.

A legacy of Nate's early days in the mountains

10

when it seemed there were man-eating grizzlies behind every tree and it was just his luck to run into each and every one, Nate was known to the tribes in the region as Grizzly Killer. "Why?" he signed. "I never set eyes on you before." He was sure of it. "What have I done that you would rub me out?"

"You are white," the young Ute signed, then lowered his hands, as if that were explanation enough.

"There are many whites in these mountains," Nate signed. Which was an exaggeration. There were a score, if that. "Why pick me?"

"You are the only white who lives on Ute land. You are the only white who has killed Utes and lived. We do not want your kind here."

"We?" from Shakespeare.

The young Ute's jaw muscles twitched, but he did not respond. Heedless of the pistols trained on him, he examined his wound, then signed, "I will live."

"You might," Shakespeare said. "You might not. Stand up. You are coming with us."

Is that smart? Nate almost asked, but didn't, for the simple reason that it was. They couldn't just leave the Ute there. The youth might try to remedy his failure at a later date.

"What is your name?" Shakespeare inquired.

"I will not tell you."

"Fine. We will make up a name of our own." Shakespeare winked at Nate. "We will call you Buffalo Droppings."

The youth sputtered in indignation. "I am Black Beak," he signed.

11

"Buffalo Droppings it is." Shakespeare bent and hauled Black Beak to his feet, then signed, "You are coming with us to Grizzly Killer's wood lodge."

"I do not want to," Black Beak sullenly signed.

Shakespeare jabbed his pistol into the exit wound, and the young warrior winced and nearly cried out. "What you want and do not want are no longer important. You are our captive and you will do as we say."

"We will kill you, too, old one, before we are done. We will kill all whites! The land will be ours again!"

"Is that what this is about? You and your friends are white-haters?"

The look Black Beak bestowed on McNair was one of utter contempt. "You make it sound like a bad thing, old one. But how many whites hate my kind for no other reason than the color of our skin?"

"You have a point," Shakespeare conceded, then bobbed his bearded chin at Nate. "But this man is not one of them. He is different from most. He is not a bigot. He has always offered the hand of friendship to the red man, your people included."

A hint of uncertainty marked Black Beak's face, but only for a second. Then it was gone, erased by the spite he radiated. "You lie, old one. Rabid Wolf says he is no different. He came to our country, he took land my people claim as their own, he lived here against our will for many winters. Stealing our land is what all whites do."

12

Nate had stood silent long enough. "Who is Rabid Wolf?"

Black Beak's lips compressed into a thin slip and he did not respond.

"We'll question him later," Shakespeare said. "Don't worry. I have a few tricks up my sleeve." He looked at the Ute and signed, "I will make you talk."

"Torture me all you want," Black Beak responded. "I will not break."

Shakespeare had to laugh. "You think highly of yourself, boy. But we are not Apaches. We do not torture people." To Nate he quipped, "Although if this peckerwood keeps treating us as if we're the south end of buffalo heading north, we might make an exception."

Just then the undergrowth to the east crackled explosively and out of it burst most of the rest of the party: Zach, Winona, Evelyn, Louisa, and Blue Water Woman.

Nate's eyes narrowed. "Where's Touch the Clouds?" No sooner did he ask than, the underbrush to the west parted and out rode the giant Shoshone, making no more noise than would a wary buck.

Touch the Clouds drew rein and coldly studied the prisoner. He had circled around in case the Ute was able to evade his friends so he would be in a position to stop him or track him and bring him back. He did not speak Ute, but like all his people he was fluent in sign language. His fingers flowed smoothly. "I am Touch the Clouds of the Shoshones." The sign for his people was actually three signs, that for Indian, that for sheep, and the sign for eat. It was a matter of considerable distaste for him that his people were known as the Sheep Eaters by other tribes.

There was a reason. In the early days, the Shoshones lived in the upper elevations of the mountains and subsisted mainly on mountain sheep, elk, and deer. Someone, somewhere, started calling them Sheep Eaters, and the name stuck. But now only a few Shoshones stuck to the high country. Most, like Touch the Clouds's band, lived in villages much like those of the Plains tribes. Buffalo was the main item in their diet, the same as the Sioux and the Cheyenne and the Arapaho. But still the Shoshones were called Sheep Eaters.

Out of his deep personal pride, Touch the Clouds said aloud in his own tongue, "I am Touch the Clouds of the Sosoni."

"The one who makes his bed with whites," Black Beak signed in scorn.

Nate could not have foreseen what happened next. He had known Touch the Clouds for almost twenty years and rarely saw his friend lose his temper, but the hulking warrior lost it now. Suddenly bending, Touch the Clouds cuffed Black Beak across the face. Not with his full strength, or he would have broken the youth's neck, but hard enough that Black Beak rocked on his heels and almost fell.

For a few moments, no one spoke or moved.

They were too shocked—Winona most of all. Her cousin had been one of her bosom childhood friends, and she regarded him as one of the finest of her people and one of the best men ever. She looked up to him as she did few others, and she would never have imagined he would hit someone who was wounded and unarmed. "Touch the Clouds?" she said in Shoshone.

"I know of these cubs," the giant warrior informed her. "I will scout and see if the rest are close by."

"The rest?" Winona said, but her cousin was already reining into the trees. She noticed her husband give her a quizzical look, and she shrugged and said in English, "I do not know what that was about."

Nate could speak Shoshone as well as any white man alive, yet he wasn't as adept at it as his wife was at English. She was a natural-born linguist, and quickly learned any language she put her mind to. The reference to "cubs" that Touch the Clouds had made puzzled him, but he could wait to question him. He turned to his son. "How is your chest?"

"I'm fine," Zach said a trifle testily. He did not like being reminded of his blunder. "I think you should let me put a bullet in his brain."

At moments like this, Nate worried about his son as only a father could. "We can't go around killing folks on general principle."

"He tried to bushwhack you," Zach noted. "Nothing general about that." Fingering his rifle, he smirked at the young Ute, who was about the same age.

"Enough talk about killing," Winona said. "We have been riding for many sleeps, and I, for one, am anxious to see our cabin again. Let us press on. Half a mile and we will be there."

Shakespeare stepped to his mare and opened a parfleche. Inside, among other items, was a coil of rope. Unwinding it, he tied Black Beak's elbows together, leaving the Ute's hands free so he could use sign language if need be. Then, holding the other end, Shakespeare climbed back onto the mare. "Ready when you are."

"Just a second." With all that had gone on, Nate had neglected to reload his Hawken—a serious lapse for which he mentally chided himself. As he had ingrained into his children when they were sprouts, a loaded weapon could mean the literal difference between life and death. A frontiersman, or frontierswoman, *always* reloaded as quickly as they could.

Evelyn kneed her mount closer for a better look at their captive. "Shouldn't we bandage him first? He must be hurting."

"At the cabin will be soon enough," Shakespeare said, marveling at her tender nature. There were days when he thought she was too kind for her own good and had no business living in the mountains.

"Some homecoming," Louisa mentioned. She, too, was eager to reach her in-laws' cabin, but only because the sooner they did, the sooner she and

Zach could head for their own. McNair and his wife had even farther to go.

"Typical," Evelyn said. "There's always someone trying to make wolf bait of us."

"Are you going to start that again?" Winona asked severely. Her daughter made no secret of her dislike for life in the wild, and many times had voiced her desire to live east of the Mississippi where, as Evelyn liked to put it, "people were not always trying to kill one another."

"No, Mother, I am not," Evelyn said. "I've learned my lesson." Her recent experiences in the States had taught her that whites were not the paragons of virtue and nobility she once believed.

Winona was going to ask what she meant, but just then Nate swung into the saddle and urged them on. She brought her mount up alongside his bay and glanced up at him. "What do you make of the attempt on your life?"

"Too soon to say yet," Nate replied.

"Some would call it a bad omen, husband."

Nate chuckled lightly. "Since when did you become superstitious? Next you'll be afraid to walk under a ladder."

"An attempt on one's life is nothing to laugh at." Call it intuition or call it a hunch, Winona had a feeling that worse was to come.

Chapter Two

The splendor of the Rocky Mountains had to be seen for their breathtaking beauty to be appreciated. Peaks that towered over two miles above sea level, crystal-clear icy emerald lakes, jagged gorges and broad canyons, ravines that seemed bottomless, cliffs so sheer that not even mountain sheep could scale them. Timber everywhere, lushly forested slopes of broad pines and tall firs and quivering aspens. Streams and rivers that gurgled their swift way to the plains and beyond.

For Nate King, it was love at first sight. That first day he set foot in the Rockies, he loved the mountains as he had never loved anywhere in his life. They fit him like a perfectly tailored suit of clothes. They fit him as the streets and alleys of New York City never had. He had come, he had stayed, and he would not forsake the mountains this side of the grave.

Nate had never known that a person could fall so passionately in love with a chunk of real estate. The thick greenery of his native New York had been fine. He had whiled away many an hour on his uncle's farm, enjoying the outdoors. But in his estimation, the verdant East could not begin to compare to the unmatched majesty of the West. The East was grand, but the West was more than grand. The West was paradise.

Everywhere there was wildlife. Nature in all her varied guises. Birds chirping gaily in the trees or fluttering on outstretched wings; sparrows, wrens, robins, jays, larks, warblers, bluebirds, woodpeckers, and others. There were deer and elk and buffalo—shaggy mountain buffalo, not their trimmer kin on the prairie far below. There were foxes and coyotes and wolves. There were bobcats and mountain lions and an occasional lynx. There were black bears in abundance and grizzlies in reduced numbers, but still far too many to make travel ever truly safe.

Above all, there was a raw vitality unique to the mountains. The pulse of life was stronger, more vibrant.

Nate thrived on the mountains as he never had on the dales and hills of the Appalachians. He had been to the desert Southwest and the mossy forest-lands of the Pacific, but they did not stir him as the Rockies stirred him. They did not reach into the marrow of his being and fill him with a zest for being alive.

This latest trek east had been emotional torture.

He did not like being gone so long. Months had passed since Nate last saw the high valley he had staked out as his own. A pristine sanctuary protected by stark peaks, with a jewel of a lake at its center.

Now, as Nate came to the crown of the last ridge and set eyes on his personal slice of heaven on earth, he smiled in heartfelt relief. They were home at long last. Truly home, where they belonged.

But no sooner had the thought flitted through Nate's mind than reality crashed down with the weight of an avalanche. Because near the lake, in the vicinity of his cabin, smoke coiled into the air. Smoke where there should not be any. Smoke from a campfire.

"We have visitors," Winona said.

Nate grimly nodded. She did not sound any happier about it than he felt. "We don't need this."

Winona knew what he meant. After their trials back east, after nearly losing their son to a hangman's noose and their daughter to an enemy's thirst for vengeance, after weeks and weeks of being on the go, of long hours each day in the saddle, of blistering heat and whipping wind, they were keenly looking forward to peace and rest and quiet.

The others came up. Shakespeare signed to Black Beak, "Are those your friends down there?"

The young warrior merely glared.

"I'll go see," Zach offered, and lifted his reins.

"No." Nate said it more sternly than he intended. His son, after all, was a grown man, with a wife and homestead of his own, and could do as he pleased. But a father could never help being a father. "Stay with Lou and the others. It's my cabin. It's mine to do."

"*Ours* to do," Winona corrected him. It was her home, as well.

Touch the Clouds kneed his big warhorse forward. "I will go with you," he said in Shoshone.

Nate opened his mouth to say it wasn't necessary but closed it again. His friend would take it as an insult. They had helped each other many times over the years. He could not justify refusing.

"Have a care, Horatio," Shakespeare advised, and raised his gaze to the sky. "Oh god of battles! Steel my soldiers' hearts! Possess them not with fear. Take from them now the sense of reckoning, if the opposed numbers pluck their hearts from them."

Evelyn giggled and said, "I love it when you quote William S., Uncle Shakespeare. I can listen to you do it all day."

"Don't encourage him." Nate clucked to his bay.

"Why, I never!" Shakespeare pretended to be offended. "His kisses are Judas's own children."

"He kisses you?" Evelyn asked.

Nate did not hear his flustered mentor's muttered answer, which was just as well. With Winona and Touch the Clouds strung out behind him, he wound lower, keeping to the heavy timber until they were near the valley floor. They were east of the lake. Across it, on the far side, was another tract of woods, and among those trees, his cabin.

"Who are they?" Winona wondered.

Eight figures ringed a fire between the lake and the woods to the west. Squatting nearby were several more. They had rigged a spit and were roasting meat. At that distance Nate couldn't tell much other than that they were Indians.

Touch the Clouds had keener eyesight. "This is strange. Some are Utes. Some are Crows. All are young. All are painted for war."

"How can that be?" Winona said. The Utes and the Crows were not on the friendliest of terms.

"We'll sort it out later," Nate said. "Right now we have to figure out how to deal with them."

Touch the Clouds had trouble with English, but he understood enough to say, "They must be killed."

"I never knew you to be so bloodthirsty," Nate mentioned.

"Rabid Wolf is not to be trusted," Touch the Clouds explained. "I heard of him before we left. They say his heart has gone bad."

Nate's frown deepened. It was the same as a white man saying another white man was a criminal. It meant Rabid Wolf had turned rogue.

"They say he hates whites," Touch the Clouds added.

"He's waiting for us to return so he can wipe us out," Nate guessed. "Black Beak was posted back along the trail to keep watch, only instead of riding here to warn Rabid Wolf, he tried to count coup on me himself."

"That is how I see it, yes," Touch the Clouds agreed.

"Nine against three," Winona noted. "Should I

go fetch Zach and Shakespeare? Lou and Evelyn can watch Black Beak."

It made sense, but after Zach's impetuous act earlier, Nate preferred not to expose his headstrong son to more peril just then. "Touch the Clouds and I will take care of them. Wait here."

"You know better, husband," Winona said.

"I can't watch your back and mine, both."

"When have I ever asked you to?" Winona never liked being treated as less than equal. "I have never let you down, and I will not start now."

Nate sighed. Arguing was pointless. When she made up her mind, there was no moving her. Besides which, she was right. "See their horses? We'll stick to cover and run them off, then have Rabid Wolf and his friends drop their weapons."

"It sounds easy enough," Winona said, but she was not optimistic. There was no predicting how Rabid Wolf would react.

"Here we go," Nate said quietly, and paralleled the tree line, hunched low to reduce his silhouette. He was struck by how much he had changed since he came to the Rockies. When he was Zach's age, he wouldn't have hesitated to ride into Rabid Wolf's camp with his rifle and pistols blazing. But here he was, going out of his way to avoid bloodshed when he had cause to believe Rabid Wolf was out for his. It showed how much he had matured.

The thought gave him a start. Was he being mature or was he being stupid? His life wasn't the only one at stake. He had his family and two of his best friends in all creation to think of.

Nate glanced at Winona, who smiled encouragingly. What in the world was he doing? he asked himself. Exposing her to danger, when the smart thing to do was to take Touch the Clouds's advice and kill as many of the hostiles as he could? He slowed, torn by indecision.

That was when three more young warriors came out of the trees on the far side of the lake, emerging from the trail that linked the lake to Nate's cabin. Drawing rein, Nate involuntarily straightened.

"Do you see what I see, husband?" Winona whispered.

Nate nodded, the hot flush of anger creeping from his neck to his brow. The newcomers were carrying some of his family's personal effects. He couldn't make it all out at that distance, but he distinctly saw a quilt Winona had made, draped over one warrior's shoulder. And another was carrying the cooking pot that normally hung in their fireplace.

"They have broken into our cabin and are stealing our things," Winona said.

A couple of years ago, during a visit to St. Louis, Nate bought a metal lock for the cabin door. Installing it had taken some doing, but soon his was the only cabin in the Rockies with that extra bit of security. No one else bothered with locks. Doorstops and door bars were used when the occupants were home, and when they weren't, anyone could walk in at any time.

Easterners thought it folly. A gent from Philadelphia once went on and on about how it was preposterous to trust in the good graces of total strangers. Nate had smiled and said that the Easterner didn't understand the difference between folks who lived in cities and towns and those who lived on farms or in the backwoods.

"Country folk are naturally more trusting," Nate had summed up his sentiments.

"Country folks are more liable to have their throats slit" was the Philadelphian's assessment.

Nate had gone on to say that Indians were just as trusting. Tepees did not have locks. They had flaps, and when a flap was down, no one would think of entering without the owner's permission. "It's a matter of personal honor."

"It's a matter of being misguided," the Philadelphian disagreed. "I don't care if you're white or you're red—if you trust your fellow man, you'll end up with a knife in the back."

Nate jabbed his heels against the bay. Any qualms of conscience he had evaporated. The sanctity of his home had been violated. So what if Rabid Wolf's band were all young and didn't know any better? He wasn't God Almighty. He couldn't peer into the depths of their souls and judge their worth, or lack thereof. He was a man, and he must take other men as they presented themselves, and the young warriors laughing and joking and having a grand old time across the lake were renegade raiders and would-be killers.

One of them had produced a beaded buckskin dress and was holding it in front of him and shaking his hips from side to side.

Winona saw him and gripped her rifle tighter. The dress was too small to be one of hers. It had to be one of Evelyn's. A garment her daughter had spent hours fashioning from doeskin under her watchful eye.

Touch the Clouds brought his big warhorse up next to Nate's bay. "Be ready, Grizzly Killer," he said. With that, without any explanation, he veered toward the lake and rode out into the open.

Dumbfounded, Nate drew rein.

"What is he doing?" Winona asked, aghast.

Touch the Clouds rode midway to the lake and reined up with his warhorse facing the camp. Raising his lance, he threw back his head and gave voice to a piercing war whoop.

Rabid Wolf's band leaped to their feet, stared a few moments, then scrambled for their horses. Presently, all twelve swept around the lake, riding bunched together, readying their weapons.

"My cousin has lost his mind," Winona said.

"No, he's crafty, like a fox." Nate gigged the bay to a shadowed patch at the edge of the trees and thumbed back the hammer on his Hawken. "Go for the ones with guns. If we're lucky, half will be dead before they know what's hit them."

The young Utes and Crows approached at a wary walk. They spread out, moving six abreast. Most had bows, arrows nocked to the sinew strings. Only one had a lance. Two had guns, older trade rifles, the kind the Hudson's Bay Company gave in exchange for prime plews.

Touch the Clouds was a statue. He sat his warhorse as impassively as if he were in the center of his village, his lance across his thighs, his features inscrutable. Nate noticed, though, that Touch the Clouds's eyes flicked from warrior to warrior, taking their measure, gauging which posed the greater threat.

"That stocky one in front must be Rabid Wolf," Winona whispered.

Nate thought so, too. The warrior in question had a square head to go with his square body. His face was hard as flint, his lips a cruel slit. Nate had seen faces like that before, on men to whom mercy and compassion were alien. Men who were natural-born killers.

Oddly, Rabid Wolf had not unslung his bow. His hands were empty save for his reins, and he made no move to draw either his knife or his tomahawk as he brought his band to a halt twenty paces out.

For the longest while, no one spoke. The young warriors studied the giant Shoshone, and some of them did not like what they saw. They fidgeted and glanced from one to the other and then at their leader.

For his part, Rabid Wolf was smiling. "What have we here?" he said in Ute, then switched to surprisingly good English. "Do you speak the tongue of the white dogs?"

"A little," Touch the Clouds said.

Nate thought of the many evenings on the trail they had spent helping him hone his fluency. Touch the Clouds was too modest by half.

"I speak it well. I also speak French. I learned

them from an old voyageur who lives in the bluff country."

This was news of interest to Nate. Voyageurs hailed from Canada and had been common in the mountains during trapping days.

"I am Rabid Wolf. I know who you are. Even among my people, the fame of Touch the Clouds has spread. They say you have counted many coup." When Touch the Clouds did not respond, Rabid Wolf went on. "They also say you are a friend to the white man I have come here to slay. They say you are blood brother to Grizzly Killer."

Touch the Clouds placed his hands on his lance. "I call him brother, yes. If you have come to rub out Grizzly Killer, it is you who will be rubbed out. Grizzly Killer has counted as many coup as I have."

Rabid Wolf was not impressed. "I heard about him growing up. I heard about how he is friend to all Indians who are friends to him. I heard of the many bears he has killed. As many as it would take ten men to kill in ten lifetimes, he has killed in one. I heard, and I did not believe."

"The stories are true," Touch the Clouds said.

"No one can kill that many bears," Rabid Wolf said. "All whites speak with two tongues."

"You are a fool, young one."

Rabid Wolf's slit of a smile vanished. "The fools are the elders of my tribe who have granted permission for Grizzly Killer to live on our land. The biggest fool of all is Neota, our leader, who has smoked the pipe of friendship with Grizzly Killer and, like you, calls him brother."

"What has Grizzly Killer done that you hate him so?" Touch the Clouds asked.

"Have you eyes but do not see? Ears but do not hear? Grizzly Killer is white. What more reason do I need?"

"Not all whites are the same. Many have two tongues, it is true, but Grizzly Killer is not one of them. He is honest and his heart is good."

"An honest white is still a white," Rabid Wolf said.

"Now I understand," Touch the Clouds said. "You are one of those who hate anyone whose skin is not as yours. You hate Grizzly Killer not because he lives on Ute land and breathes Ute air, but because he is white."

"Have I said differently?" Rabid Wolf retorted. "I am not ashamed of my hate. I am proud to hate whites. They have brought hardship to many tribes. They have taken land that does not belong to them. They have killed game that was not theirs to kill. We must drive them from the mountains while we can. Before they grow in number and sweep all before them like a swarm of locusts."

"How many whites have you killed?"

"Seven. A white man and a white woman in a wooden lodge to the south, and five whites in long dresses who did not lift a finger to defend themselves but fell on their knees and held their hands like this." Rabid Wolf clasped his as if in prayer. "They would not fight back no matter what we did."

"I have met such whites. They are called missionaries. They walk with the Great Mystery."

"They were cowards," Rabid Wolf spat. "They would rather die than spill blood. Killing them was like killing baby birds."

"Yet you did it anyway."

"I would do it again. I would do it until there are no more whites left. Until the mountains are free of their kind. Until our land is ours again."

Touch the Clouds brought up something Nate was wondering about. "Voyageurs are white, are they not? How is it the one who taught you the white tongue is still alive?"

"He is the one white I cannot kill," Rabid Wolf said, but he did not elaborate.

One of the other young Utes straightened and spoke in the Ute language. Nate was not as fluent in Ute as he was in Shoshone, but he knew enough to translate what was said. "Why all this talk? Are we women or warriors? Let us rub this one out and be done."

"Patience, Little Hawk," Rabid Wolf said. "It is a great honor to meet so famous a warrior. He is a Shoshone and he is our enemy. But a man can respect his enemies as well as his friends." He repeated what he had said in English.

"You speak of honor, yet you do not honor the words of your elders," Touch the Clouds pointed out. "You do not leave Grizzly Killer in peace as they want."

"They are old and live by the old ways. I am young and live by my own ways. And I say all whites must be driven from the mountains or moisten its ground with their blood."

Touch the Clouds squared his wide shoulders. "I ask you, young one, as one warrior to another. Let Grizzly Killer and his family live in peace.

"You ask too much, Shoshone."

"I ask only that which is right." Touch the Clouds regarded the rest of them. "Go. Now. Or many of you will die."

"I expect better of you," Rabid Wolf said. "You are one and we are many, and many always win over one."

"A bear is one and bees are many, but that does not stop the bear from eating their honey," Touch the Clouds said. "A bull elk is one and a pack of wolves are many, but with my own eyes I have seen a bull elk drive off many hungry wolves."

Rabid Wolf glanced right and left, and grinned. In Ute he said, "Be ready, my brothers. Soon we will cut off his nose and his ears to take back and show our people."

A tall, lanky Crow kneed his horse forward. "I do not like this, Rabid Wolf," he said in sign language. "We agreed to help you fight whites. Not to fight Shoshone chiefs. Touch the Clouds is bad medicine. He is hard to kill. I know. My people have tried many times."

"That does not surprise me," Little Hawk signed. "Your people are poor warriors. It takes five of you to kill a frog."

"You dare!" The Crow's right hand dropped to a knife at his hip.

Before he could draw it, Rabid Wolf reined between them. "Enough!" he signed. "Have you forgotten our promise to one another, Swift Snake? We must work together to drive the whites out."

"I agreed to work with you," the Crow signed, and scowled at Little Hawk. "Not this other."

Little Hawk bristled. "Everyone knows Crows do not like to fight. Their men are all women."

Swift Snake angrily raised his hand to respond, but Rabid Wolf beat him to it. "I said enough! Crows are fine warriors. They have much territory. Others have tried to take it, but the Crows are still there."

"My people are strong," Swift Snake boasted. "You Utes have tried to run us off but could not. The Bloods raid our villages, but we drive them off. Even the Sioux fear us."

A derisive snort from Little Hawk caused Swift Snake to glower. Five other Crows moved up on either side of him. Other Utes moved closer to Swift Snake. For the moment, at least, the hostiles had forgotten about Touch the Clouds.

"Perhaps they will kill one another off and save us the trouble," Winona whispered hopefully.

Wishful thinking, Nate reflected. He would like to learn more about their alliance. Was it a random happenstance, or did it betoken a new partnership that boded ill for neighboring tribes?

Touch the Clouds, all this while, sat perfectly still, one hand on his lance. He did not exploit the schism in the renegade ranks. He was waiting for them to make the first overt move of aggression.

Winona knew that. She bubbled with worry. Worry for her cousin and worry for her husband, but not for herself. She loved them both, loved them dearly, and refused to countenance the thought of being without either. She only wished Zach and the McNairs were there to even the odds.

Then movement registered out of the corner of Winona's eye. Part of her wish was being granted. Shakespeare and Zach were trotting toward Touch the Clouds. As yet the hostiles had not noticed them.

Winona was both glad and upset. Glad because the extra guns were needed, upset because even though her son was a grown man he was still first and foremost the fruit of her womb and she did not want him placed in harm's path. She glanced at Nate to see if he had noticed, and she saw that he had and he did not like it.

"I told them to stay back."

A moot point, since they hadn't, and now one of the young Utes pointed and shouted. The Utes and the Crows ended their argument and turned, as one, to confront the approaching twosome.

"So you are not alone!" Rabid Wolf snarled at Touch the Clouds. "You have brought your friends! How many more are with you?" And with that, he twisted toward the trees and looked straight at Nate and Winona.

Chapter Three

Nate King sensed what Rabid Wolf would do before Rabid Wolf did it—namely, screech in raw fury in Ute, "There in the trees! They will shoot us from hiding! Ride for your lives, my brothers!"

One of the other Utes had other ideas. He whipped his bow up, drew back the string, and sighted down the shaft.

Quick as he was, Touch the Clouds was quicker. The giant Shoshone's right arm was a blur as the long lance streaked from his hand. It caught the young Ute full in the chest at the exact instant he released the arrow. The jolt of the lance tearing through his body spoiled his aim and the arrow thudded into the earth. A second later, he thudded down beside it.

Forty yards out, Zach King whooped for joy. Battle, to him, was an emotional elixir. It set his blood to racing. Tucking his rifle to his shoulder, he fired. A Crow clutched at his head and toppled.

The rest of the hostiles were breaking for cover.

Nate slapped his legs against the bay and exploded from the woods. Winona was right by his side. An arrow missed his neck by a whisker, and he responded with the Hawken and saw the warrior topple. Another shaft whizzed past, and his wife's rifle cracked.

Winona had been trying to get a clear shot at Rabid Wolf. But the wily stripling had swung onto the off side of his warhorse and was riding hell-bent for safety toward the west end of the lake. Only his foot and part of one leg and arm showed. She rose higher and drew one of her pistols and tried to fix a bead on his arm, thinking to knock him off his horse. Too late, she spied another warrior with a bow who had chosen her as his target. Too late, she tried to shift and shoot him.

The arrow pierced Winona's upper left arm. She cried out, not meaning to, and then nearly doubled over from the pain. She would have fallen had she not grabbed her mount's mane.

Nate saw the bloody barbed point of a shaft jutting from his wife's arm and went berserk. In a rush he was in among the hostiles, swinging his rifle right and left. He hit one warrior, and another, and then he was next to the one who had shot Winona. Nate struck him not once but twice, smashing the stock against the warrior's head. A Crow sheared a knife at Nate's abdomen, and he jerked aside and countered with a swing that nearly caved in the Crow's face.

Letting go of the Hawken, Nate drew both pistols. He cocked them as he swept them up and out. He shot a warrior in the heart, swiveled, and shot another who was about to put an arrow in his back.

Then Touch the Clouds was there, his long knife flashing. Zach and Shakespeare were closing, firing as they came. The hostiles near Nate seemed to melt into the air, freeing him to rush to Winona's side and loop an arm about her waist. "Watch the arm. I'll lower you down."

Winona was embarrassed. Not because she was wounded. That was to be expected in battle. She was ashamed because she had cried out. Because to her way of thinking, she had shown weakness. From an early age, Shoshone girls were taught to be worthy of their warrior men. Women must never, never wail or scream or betray fear in the presence of an enemy. "I can manage, husband."

"Like hell," Nate said gruffly. The arrow had skewed her arm like a spit through a haunch of venison. Bright drops of blood dripped from the tip as he carefully dismounted while easing her to the ground.

Winona grit her teeth in frustration. Not only had she screamed, her legs were weak. She tried to stand and nearly buckled at the knees. "I am sorry."

"For what?" Nate responded. "For getting hit?" He was between her and the hostiles, screening her with his body. A yip caused him to whip around. He thought they were about to be attacked, but it was a retreating Ute who had shrieked in baffled outrage as he and his fellows fled before Touch the Clouds, Zach, and Shakespeare.

Four bodies littered the ground. Three were still, but the fourth warrior was still alive and feebly groaning, his chest spurting a fine scarlet mist.

"I let you down," Winona said through clenched teeth. Had it not been for her, they could have slain the entire band.

"What are you babbling about?" Nate couldn't understand why she was so upset. The remaining hostiles were in full flight. Rabid Wolf had already disappeared into the distant trees. Zach and Touch the Clouds were pursuing them, but Shakespeare had turned back.

"How bad is it?" the white-haired mountaineer asked as he reined up.

"I don't know yet." Nate wanted to examine Winona's arm, but she was leaning her forehead against him, her face pale and slick with sweat.

Licking her lips, Winona said again, "I am sorry."

Shakespeare sprang down to lend his aid and help ease her onto her back. "What does she have to be sorry about?"

"Beats me." Nate figured she was in shock and did not know what she was saying. That happened sometimes. "I thought you were supposed to stay back and let us handle this."

"When your son saw Touch the Clouds ride into the open, a herd of buffalo couldn't hold him back. He wanted in on the bloodletting." Shakespeare paused. "You know how he gets."

Yes, Nate did, and he would talk to his son about it, but first things first. He bent over his wife's arm. "It missed the bone, and you're not bleeding that much."

"She was lucky," Shakespeare said. He had seen many a man left crippled by such a wound. Or else they died from loss of blood.

"Lucky?" Winona repeated, and would have laughed if her stomach were not churning. She did not feel lucky. She felt stupid. "Remove it. I do not want my daughter to see me like this."

Nate was examining the point for telltale traces of poison. Some tribes dipped their arrows into the livers of dead animals or used rattlesnake venom. The Utes were not known to do either, and the barb was not discolored in any way. "I'll have to break it."

Winona nodded. The pain was growing worse. Dark fingers plucked at her mind, but she refused to pass out. That would be the ultimate indignity. Tossing her head to clear it, she said, "Do what you must, husband."

From the distant woods came a gunshot. Shakespeare debated going to help Zach and Touch the Clouds, but by the time he caught up it would be over. It upset him to think that some of the hostiles were bound to get away and try to kill them another day.

"Great homecoming we're having," Nate muttered. He had looked forward to peace and tranquillity. They needed it after all they had been through.

"Don't worry," Shakespeare said, and quoted, "'Tis not so deep as a well, nor so wide as a church-door." He affectionately patted Winona's right hand. "You'll be good as can be in a month."

"The arrow, you mean?" Nate said, realizing his mentor had misunderstood.

"What else, Horatio? Or are you railing against fate? Whether 'tis nobler in the mind to suffer the slings and arrows of outrageous fortune?" Shakespeare smiled. "Trust me. It isn't."

Nate ignored him. With both hands he gingerly grasped the arrow below the point. The shaft was slick with Winona's blood. "Brace yourself," he cautioned her.

"Do what you must," Winona repeated. Her temples were throbbing and her mouth had gone as dry as sand.

His shoulders bunching, Nate steadied his left hand and tensed his right. He had to break the shaft cleanly and quickly or he would add to her suffering. "I love you," he said, and did it.

At the *snap*, Winona nearly cried out a second time. New torment flooded through her. Although Nate had done his best to hold the arrow steady, it felt as if the shaft had scraped her bone. Her queasiness grew. The world spun, and she had to close her eyes to keep from passing out.

"Are you all right?" Nate asked. Causing her pain, however inadvertently, horrified him.

"Finish," Winona urged, and braced herself.

Nate looked at Shakespeare, who nodded. He switched his left hand to the rear half of the arrow and slowly began pulling, holding the arrow as steady as he could. "Any moment now."

It could not be soon enough for Winona. She could feel the shaft sliding out of her, feel it passing through her flesh. She was on the cusp of collapsing when Nate exhaled. The job was done. He held the arrow a moment, scowling, then cast it aside with a savage gesture.

"They will die for hurting you. Every last one of them."

The drum of hooves caused Shakespeare to pivot. "Here come the others. They must figure it's safe."

Evelyn and Blue Water Woman were approaching at a gallop. Louisa was farther back, leading Black Beak by the rope.

"Doesn't anyone ever listen to me?" Nate groused. He had told them to wait until he signaled.

"They're females," Shakespeare said. "They only listen when they want to, and they never want to."

"I heard that," Winona said.

McNair chortled and tenderly touched her cheek. "It's nice to see that you don't let a little thing like being shot with an arrow spoil your sense of humor."

Winona forced her head to rise and her mouth to crease in a smile. "How little would you think it was if they had put an arrow in your arm?"

"Oh, heavens," Shakespeare said. "I'd be blubbering my brains out. Men are big babies at heart."

"Speak for yourself," Nate said stiffly. He was in no mood for lighthearted banter. Not with his wife in anguish and his son off after those who had harmed her.

"In troth, I think I should. And undo it when I had done." Rising, Shakespeare stepped to his mare and opened a parfleche. "I can keep honest counsel, ride, run, mar a curious tale in telling it, and deliver a plain message bluntly. That which ordinary men are fit for, I am qualified in, and the best of me is diligence."

"In plain English, if you please," Nate said.

Shakespeare produced a strip of buckskin. "Use this to bandage her until we get to your place. It's all I have left of an old shirt I once cut up for situations like this one."

Winona shook her head. "I can manage until we get there."

"You'll do as we say," Nate declared, and drew his Bowie to cut the sleeve of her buckskin dress. She tried to pull her arm away, and winced. "Serves you right," Nate said. "Now, stop being pigheaded and lie still."

"That's the way," Shakespeare said. "Women love it when men sweet-talk them like that. I could take lessons from you."

"You can jump off a cliff," Nate said. He was all set to slice his blade into the buckskin when the hammering of hooves reached a crescendo and his daughter vaulted from her horse and practically threw herself at Winona.

"Mother! You're hurt!"

Winona enfolded Evelyn in her good arm and held her close, the pounding in her temples now mimicked by the pounding of her heart. "I am all right, little one," she said softly, shaken by how close she had come to never holding her again.

"You are not all right." This from Blue Water Woman, who knelt to inspect the wound. To Nate she said, "We will look after her. You should check on the others."

Nate almost told her that he would look after his wife himself, but Blue Water Woman enjoyed a fine reputation among her own people, the Flatheads, as a healer. Reluctantly, he rose, sheathed his Bowie, and moved to where he had dropped his rifle. "Take her to the cabin. I'll be there as soon as I can."

Shakespeare gripped the reins to his mare. "That makes two of us, Horatio."

"No, it doesn't," Nate snapped. "Stay with the women. And this time I mean *stay* with them. There might be more hostiles around, or Rabid Wolf might circle back." He climbed on the bay. "We're taking too much for granted these days."

"Is that experience speaking?" Shakespeare asked.

Nate grunted. They both knew it was. "If you need me, fire two shots into the air, one right after the other. I'll hear them anywhere in the valley."

"Watch your back, Horatio."

"Always." Nate wasted no more time, but galloped to where the hostiles had fled into the woods. Their tracks were plain enough for a ten-year-old to follow. He pushed on, moving as swiftly as the terrain allowed, alert for sign of his son or Touch the Clouds.

Half a mile to the west, Zach King was about to rein past a rock outcropping when suddenly Touch the Clouds was beside him and motioning sharply for him to halt. Zach was going to ask why, but Touch the Clouds motioned for him not to speak, then pointed at a dense stand of firs.

Zach started to look when, without warning, he was struck in the shoulder by a blow so powerful, it knocked him from the saddle. He thought he had been shot and pressed his hand to his shoulder. Only, there was no wound and no blood. Because there was no bullet hole.

Touch the Clouds was beside him, flat on his stomach. The Shoshone tapped him and pointed again, this time at a tree behind them. A quivering arrow was embedded inches in the trunk.

Zach understood. A renegade in the firs had loosed an arrow, and only Touch the Clouds's swift thinking, and a hard push, had saved him. "Thank you," he whispered in Shoshone, but Touch the Clouds was already in motion, snaking to the left and a patch of high weeds.

Zach snaked to the right. Their horses had gone a dozen yards more and stopped. From where he lay, his sorrel blocked his view of the firs. He couldn't tell where the bowman might be. For all he knew, the man was crawling toward them. Or maybe he had lit a shuck for parts unknown.

Zach glanced at the spot where he had last seen Touch the Clouds, but the Shoshone was gone. Zach angled to a log, then cautiously raised his head high enough to peer over it. Not so much as a leaf or a pine needle stirred.

Zach stayed where he was. The trick to hunting, whether the prey had four legs or two, was patience. The best hunters were those best able to outwait whatever or whomever they were after.

A fly buzzed Zach's head. Somewhere off in the forest, a jay squawked. Somewhere nearer a sparrow chirped.

Abruptly, the sparrow rose from the firs, its wings fluttering as it frantically sought to gain altitude. Something had spooked it. A smaller sparrow, its mate, also took wing. Below them was a thicket. Zach stared long and hard, and after several minutes came to the conclusion that the base of the thicket was darker than it should be. Something, or someone, was huddled down low, and it did not take any great leap of imagination to guess who.

Zach slowly worked his way around the log. He was alert for twigs or dry leaves or anything else that might give him away. So alert, he missed the muted twang of a bowstring. But he didn't miss the arrow that sliced into the dank earth under his very nose.

Zach trained his rifle on the thicket, but the dark shape was no longer there. The renegade had changed position. He mentally swore at himself for being so careless. Rolling to the right, he slid under a small pine and froze. Now he had to hope he spotted the warrior before the warrior spotted him.

The seconds dragged into minutes and the minutes into a quarter of an hour. Zach did not see the warrior or Touch the Clouds. It occurred to him that the warrior was deliberately delaying them to give the others time to get away. He started to inch out from under the pine, then froze again. A pair of legs had appeared twenty feet away, moving slowly from north to south. They were too thin to be Touch the Clouds's. As Zach watched, the man bent at the knees and intently surveyed the vegetation in the vicinity of the log.

It was a Crow. Zach could not help but note how young he was. Sixteen, if that. No more than a kid playing at being a full-fledged warrior. But there was nothing playful about the bow the Crow held, or the arrow nocked to the string.

Zach leveled his rifle. At that distance, he couldn't miss. He took aim and started to thumb back the hammer.

Suddenly, the young Crow whirled—not toward Zach, but in the other direction. He had the bowstring halfway to his cheek when a gigantic figure heaved out of the underbrush and a hand the size of a ham connected with the side of the young Crow's head. He staggered, but gamely held on to his bow and tried to bring it to bear.

Touch the Clouds towered over the youth like a redwood over a fern. His arm swept down. Oaken sinews smashed the Crow to the earth, transforming him into a limp heap. The power in that blow was incredible.

"You can come out, Stalking Coyote," Touch the Clouds said in Shoshone, using Zach's Shoshone name. He gazed toward the small pine and beckoned.

"How did you know where I was?" Zach crawled out from underneath and unfurled. "I had no idea where you were."

"What is it your father likes to say? Experience seems to be more than it is to those who do not have it?"

"I could live to be a hundred and still not be as good as you," Zach remarked. Touch the Clouds was one of the three or four men he most admired in the world.

"You are a skilled warrior in your own right," the giant said, then reached down, gripped the Crow by the back of the neck, and casually flipped him over. "I will dispose of this one." He palmed his knife.

"Wait," Zach heard himself say, much to his surprise. Part of him was eager to slay the young Crow where he lay.

"He is our enemy," Touch the Clouds reminded him.

"An enemy in no shape to do us harm," Zach said. "I imagine my father will want to talk to him."

"There is a time for talking and a time for killing." But Touch the Clouds replaced his knife. "Take him if you want. I will ride on and be sure

Rabid Wolf and his friends have left your father's valley."

Zach would rather do that himself, but he was the one who had suggested keeping the Crow alive. "I doubt that bastard will ever show his face again after the licking we gave him."

Touch the Clouds went into the firs and reappeared leading a pinto. "You will want this," he said. Running to his big warhorse, he vaulted astride it as easily as Zach might vault a broomstick, and was off at a trot.

"The best of the Shoshones," Zach said softly. A groan reminded him that he must not let down his guard. Hunkering, he frisked the Crow, relieving him of a knife and a tomahawk, both of which he wedged under his belt. He used his own knife to cut whangs from his buckskin shirt, then tied them end to end and bound the Crow's wrists. As he stepped back, the young warrior's eyes snapped open.

The Crow started to rise, discovered he was tied, and glared at the rifle Zach had leveled. He said something in the Crow language and, when Zach did not respond, changed to English. "White Dog's son! Cut free!"

"Dream on," Zach said. "But I'll gladly slit your throat if you give me cause." He should do it anyway, but strangely enough, he did not feel the urge. "How is it you speak the white tongue?"

"White man teach. He live mother's sister. Stay village five winters when me small." The young Crow spat in the dirt. "Me not want learn. Mother

47

make. Her say good be like whites. Stupid woman!"

"That's no way to talk about your mother. Do you have a name? Or do I just call you Dumb as a Stump?"

The young Crow jutted his chin defiantly. "Me Chases Rabbits." He puffed out his skinny chest. "Maybe you hear me name? Me count plenty coup. Me great Crow warrior."

Zach laughed. "Your people are terrible liars. If you've counted coup even once, I am a she-bear." The other wasn't much more than a boy, and was probably never on a raid in his life until he hooked up with Rabid Wolf. Zach motioned for him to stand.

"Me count coup," Chases Rabbits insisted. "Come close count coup you. Touch the Clouds stop me."

"You know his name?"

"All people live mountains know great Shoshone," Chases Rabbits said. "Him famous like Long Hair, Black Elk."

"Never heard of them," Zach said, when, in truth, he knew that Long Hair was a Crow chief of considerable repute, and Black Elk a Crow warrior who once held off a Piegan raiding party long enough for his fellow warriors to rally and drive the raiders off.

Chases Rabbits was smarter than his years. "You speak two tongues, Grizzly Killer son." Awkwardly standing, he shuffled to his pinto. "What now? Me no climb on." He held out his bound wrists.

"Sure you can, if you try real hard," Zach said. "Unless you want to ride belly down."

"Me remember this." Chases Rabbits gave a high hop and swung half over the pinto. He started to slide back off but levered his right leg up and around, arresting his fall. Then, mumbling under his breath, he slowly straightened. "You not think me do, eh?" he beamed.

"I couldn't care less one way or the other," Zach answered. The Crow's attitude grated on him. "Sit there and don't move until I say so." Keeping Chases Rabbits covered, he backed toward his sorrel.

"Me no hurry die," Chases Rabbits said. "Wait others come. We swear blood oath. Help one another."

"Let them try. There can't be many left."

"Enough," Chases Rabbits said. "They do what Rabid Wolf say. Do what we come do."

"Murder us, you mean."

"Drive all whites out," Chases Rabbits declared. "Make mountains like should be. No whites anywhere."

"You'll never scare my father off," Zach said with pronounced pride.

"Then vultures eat flesh. His flesh, his woman's flesh, your flesh, your woman's flesh, your sister's flesh. Soon all no more. Soon all die."

Chapter Four

"Oh my," Winona King said.

"How could they?" Evelyn had tears in her eyes. "This is our *home!*"

Nate King was speechless. He expected to find something like this, but it still shocked him. The wonder of it was that, given all the times his family had been away for long spells, it hadn't happened before.

Their cabin door, partially splintered, hung from one hinge. Their window, the precious glass pane he had carted all the way from St. Louis, lay in dozens of glittering shards in the afternoon sunlight. A broken chair, the culprit, lay amid the glass. But it was not their only possession to litter the grass. Ripped clothes, torn blankets, shredded quilts, a shattered lamp, and a badly dented pot were just a few of the many.

"They destroyed everything," Winona said, the

ache in her bosom almost more than she could bear. She loved their cabin, the only home she had ever known other than the buffalo-hide lodges she was raised in. The curtains, the way the furniture had been arranged, the decorations, the quilts, everything in the cabin down to the tiniest detail, was *her*. An expression of her love for her family. It crushed her beyond measure to see one of her innermost fears come true.

Zach slid from the bay, his fists clenched. He had spent the greater part of his life here. He had many fond memories of happy winter nights spent listening to his father read while he was stretched out in front of the warm fireplace. Memories of carefree summer nights when they would climb onto the roof to gaze at the stars and talk about everything under the sun. He glared at Chases Rabbits. "You call yourselves warriors?" he spat.

"Rabid Wolf's idea, not me," the young Crow said defensively.

"You ride with him. You share the blame." Zach picked up a punctured water skin. "I should break both your arms. Or better yet, gut you and hang you from a tree by your intestines."

"Me not afraid," Chases Rabbits said, but he did not sound particularly fearless. "Try hurt me!"

"Hush, boy," Shakespeare McNair said, wearily dismounting. He was thinking of his own cabin and wondering if the hostiles had paid it a visit before they came to Nate's. He posed the question to their captives.

Black Beak did not respond, but Chases Rabbits

was the talkative type. "Your lodge. Breed lodge. Grizzly Killer lodge. All same."

"What?" Zach dropped the water skin and spun. "You did this to my cabin, too?" Fury bubbling within him, he seized the Crow by the arm and flung him to the ground, hard.

Chases Rabbits hit on his right shoulder and grimaced in pain. Before the Crow could sit up, Zach was on him, drawing his knife.

"You're dead, you son of a bitch!"

"Zach, don't!" Louisa shouted, and was off her horse in a twinkling. Darting over, she grabbed her husband's wrist. "Killing him would make you no better than they are."

"See if you feel the same when you see our cabin," Zach said bitterly. But he stayed his hand.

Winona reached the front door before Nate. He heard her gasp, and then a low mew such as a kitten might make.

"Oh, husband! Look at what they have done."

It was a shambles. A complete and utter shambles. Broken and torn articles were scattered all over the floor. The heavy table he had made with his own hands had been smashed to bits. The buffalo head he had mounted above their fireplace only the year before was a ruin. Their rocking chair was in fragments. But that was not the worst.

Nate moved past Winona and gaped dully at the corner where his bookcase had stood. His bookcase and his prized collection of books were no more. The shelves had been reduced to kindling, the books reduced to bits and pieces. Nate groaned and placed his hand against the wall.

"I never—" Winona said, but she did not finish what she was going to say.

"We'll have to start over," Nate said, and was hit by the full enormity of what that meant. Unwilling to endure the spectacle, he turned to go back out and nearly bumped into Evelyn, who stood in the doorway, quietly weeping.

"How could they?" she asked, but she was not addressing either of them. "We never did them any harm."

"It never pays to get too attached to our possessions," Shakespeare commented, and received a blistering glance from his wife.

"If I were to take your favorite pipe and throw it in a river," Blue Water Woman said, "you would jump in after it."

"I probably would," Shakespeare conceded with a lopsided grin. "But that just shows I'm as addlepated as the rest of the human race."

Evelyn picked a path through the debris to her bedroom. Her door, too, had been caved in, and her effects, too, were in a shambles. The dresses she had spent so many hours sewing. The bed her father had made for her, destroyed. Duck feathers everywhere, feathers that had once been in her mattress. She stepped over a splintered dresser drawer, seeking the one thing she cherished most. "Oh, no," she said quietly, and had to blink back a fresh torrent of tears.

53

The first doll she had ever been given, the Shoshone doll she'd had since she was barely able to walk, lay in pieces. She had spent many a childhood hour playing with that doll, and many a night cuddling it close as she drifted off to sleep. She had almost taken it with her but decided a girl her age should not play with dolls anymore. Besides, she figured it would be safer at the cabin. "And now look," Evelyn said aloud as she bent and gently lifted the doll's crushed head in the palm of her hand.

From the doorway Winona watched her daughter a moment more, then turned to what was left of her own personal effects and rummaged through the ruins, searching for anything that might have been spared. There was precious little. An old dress in a corner of a closet. A pair of moccasins in need of repair. A pillow they had overlooked. In the main room she found silverware and a few pots and pans. Gradually, the pile of items they could salvage grew.

Nate went back out. He had seldom been so mad. Or so upset at himself. Logic told him there was nothing he could have done to prevent it, but logic was often eclipsed by emotion when the heart was involved. He truly loved their place. It was a slice of joy carved out of the raw wilderness.

"Keep an eye on the Ute and the Crow," Nate said to Zach, and went into the trees to be alone with his thoughts. He was not alone long.

"Wait up, Horatio." Shakespeare had his Hawken in the crook of his left elbow and his right thumb hooked in his wide leather belt. "You're taking this hard, son. Harder than you should."

"Evelyn had it right. It's our *home*," Nate stressed.

"The cabin is still standing, isn't it? And you have enough money squirreled away to replace whatever you lost." Shakespeare hoped he would be as reasonable when he got to his own cabin. It was always easier to offer advice to others than to take one's own.

"That's not the point," Nate said. Coming to a shoulder-high boulder, he leaned against it and hung his head. "I didn't do enough. I let my family down. Did you see my daughter's face?"

"She's a fine young lady. She'll get over this."

"What was it you told me once?" Nate said, then remembered. "Thou art so leaky that we must leave thee to thy sinking."

Shakespeare blinked. "So it's comes to this? Having my quotes thrown back at me. Remember the one from earlier?" He paused. "To be, or not to be, that is the question. Whether 'tis nobler in the mind to suffer the slings and arrows of outrageous fortune, or to take arms against a sea of trouble, and by opposing end them."

"One of my favorites," Nate said.

"Mine too. Verily, old William S. had a flair for the language."

Nate stared off into the trees and was silent awhile. "They ripped up all my books. Every last one."

"They what? Damn them." Shakespeare

frowned. "I do smell all horse piss, at which my nose is in great indignation."

"It took me years to collect those volumes," Nate lamented. "Cooper. Byron. That Bible with the gold lettering. All gone."

"Any scoundrel who will destroy a book is a scoundrel worth hanging," Shakespeare declared. "But to them it's just so much paper and chicken scratchings."

"I don't blame them as much as you might think. They're bigots, and bigots are vile, but their hatred is understandable," Nate said. "No, I blame myself more than I do them."

Shakespeare's eyebrows pinched together. "This should be interesting. How, pray tell, is it your fault?"

"I live here."

McNair blinked again. "Oh, well, of course, how could I have overlooked that? You're to blame for them destroying everything you own because your cabin happened to be on the same planet? Makes perfect sense now that I think about it." He snapped his fingers. "Why, a lot more is clear to me, too. The British attacked us in 1812 because America is *here*. And Xerxes attacked Greece because it was *there*. And Satan hates God because God is here and there and everywhere. It's all so simple."

"Sarcasm ill becomes you."

"Oh, I like that. May I quote you as I do William S.?" Shakespeare sighed and shook his head.

"Blaming yourself for this is like a wren blaming itself for the rain that gets its feathers wet."

"You're missing my point." Nate hunkered, his rifle against his shoulder, and picked up a twig and stuck it in a corner of his mouth. "It's not as if I didn't know a lot of Utes are unhappy about a white man living in their territory. Sure, there's been a truce, but a couple of good deeds can't erase years of hostility."

"Go on," Shakespeare urged when Nate stopped.

"Look at how close we are to the prairie. A couple of hours riding and we're out of the foothills. Well-marked trails lead right to our doorsteps. It's not as if anyone couldn't find us if they wanted. Think of all the whites who have happened by. Many of whom brought us no end of trouble."

"You're leading up to something."

"The Shoshones, the Crows, the Utes, the Flatheads, the Nez Percé, they all know where we live. Hellfire, even the Blackfeet Confederacy know, and they want us rubbed out in the worst way."

"So?"

"So why did we go on living here knowing something like this was bound to happen? Why did we put ourselves in a position where it *can* happen?"

Shakespeare pursed his lips, then said, "Wait a minute, Horatio. By 'we' you're not just talking about you and your family, are you?"

"I mean *all* of us. Me and my family and Zach and Lou and you and Blue Water Woman. It's gotten so the army came right to Zach's doorstep when they were hunting him down."

"They showed up at my place first," Shakespeare remarked. "About shocked me out of six months' growth, and at my age I can't spare a single minute."

"There you have it. Now do you see why I'm as much to blame as the hostiles? If I lived somewhere else, somewhere deeper in the mountains, somewhere they couldn't find so easily, it would be different."

Now it was Shakespeare who hunkered and thoughtfully regarded the man he regarded as the son he never had. "Are you suggesting what I suspect you're suggesting? And if so, where exactly did you have in mind?"

Nate shrugged. "I haven't thought that far ahead. But there are whole sections of the Rockies we haven't seen yet. Sections no tribe claims as its own. Places off the beaten path, as it were."

Shakespeare gazed at the peaks to the west. "Move deeper into the mountains? All of us together?"

"Why not? For our mutual protection, if no other reason. There has to be a suitable spot. A valley like this one, only big enough for all of us to have elbow space. A valley no other whites or Indians have set eyes on."

"Horatio, you astound me," Shakespeare confessed. "You expect a gent my age to uproot himself and move all I have?"

"I would help. And who are you joshing? You

have plenty of years left, and more energy than most coons half your age."

"Flattery won't work on me," Shakespeare said, chuckling.

"All I ask is that you think about the idea," Nate proposed, "and if you decide it's a notion worth pursuing, we'll scout around for a likely spot."

Shakespeare ran a hand through his white beard. "Even if I go along with the idea, there are two big obstacles. They go by the names of Blue Water Woman and Winona. My wife likes living close to her people and your wife likes living close to hers. Persuading them to go off into the unknown will take some doing. Then there's Zach and Lou. He might not want to live within spitting distance of us."

"It won't be as if he were right next door." But Nate had to admit his friend had a point. Zach was at the age where he liked to be on his own, the age where young men stretched their wings to find out how high they could fly.

"There's a lot to be said for living near the Shoshones and the Flatheads," Shakespeare had gone on. "It's nice to have them handy if they're needed."

"We can still visit them whenever we want," Nate said.

Shakespeare raised his hands. "Don't waste your breath on me. It's the women you'll have to convince, and that could take some doing."

"Maybe so," Nate allowed, but to him it was worth the effort. The more he considered it, the more the idea appealed to him. "A valley all to ourselves," he said wistfully. "Where the outside world can't intrude. Where things like this won't happen." He indicated his cabin.

"Nothing is ever etched in stone, Horatio," Shakespeare said. "Don't expect to find heaven. We live below the clouds, not above them."

"The notion is worth pursuing," Nate insisted. He had more to say, but just then the undergrowth crackled to the passage of a horse and rider and into view trotted Touch the Clouds on his warhorse. The giant warrior was making a beeline for the cabin but spotted them and reined over as they rose to greet him.

"I was about ready to come looking for you," Shakespeare said.

Touch the Clouds rested his lance across his legs. "I followed their sign to the high pass to the southwest. They have left the valley."

"Good riddance," Nate said in English. In Shoshone he said, "I thank you, my friend. For coming with us to St. Louis. For helping out when I was mauled by the black bear. For being there when we needed you."

"You are family," Touch the Clouds said simply.

"Would it upset you if we moved away?"

"Move where? Back to the white world?"

"No. Ten or twenty sleeps into the mountains. Maybe more," Nate said. "I am tired of trouble showing up at my lodge."

Touch the Clouds tilted his head quizzically. "You must do as you think best, Grizzly Killer. No matter how far you move, it would not stop our hearts from being one. We are blood brothers. We will always be blood brothers. Just as Winona will always be my cousin."

Nate was touched. "You are as fine a man as I have ever met, red or white."

"I am no better or worse than most, Grizzly Killer," Touch the Clouds responded. "Now I must give Winona and Evelyn a hug and be on my way. I have been gone from my people much too long." He smiled and tapped his heels against his mount.

"I reckon we should get back, too," Shakespeare said, arching his spine to relieve a cramp. "How soon do you need an answer about moving?"

"There's no rush," Nate said, "but I aim to start looking for a new home tomorrow if I can."

"That soon? You really are serious about this, aren't you?" McNair moved into the clearing. "Ever been northwest of here about twenty-five or thirty miles as the crow flies? And half a mile higher?"

"Plenty of times. Why?"

"Covered every square inch, have you?" Shakespear's eyes sparkled. "Once, in my younger days, when I was trapping for a living, I stumbled on a valley high up where I didn't think one would be. Pretty place. Had a lake with green water."

"Green as in grass?"

"Greenish blue as in the color of some ice up on a high peak. A glacier, I believe it's called. Leftover from ancient times when this part of the country had winter all year long."

61

"I've seen a few," Nate mentioned. But always from a distance. Glaciers were invariably difficult to reach, because they were always at or near the very tops of the mountains.

Shakespeare said, "Indians don't go up that high much except to hunt in the spring and the fall."

"You're saying this valley is worth a look-see?"

"If you can find it, you might like it. I don't recall there being a sign humans ever set foot in it before me. I was only there one night, you understand, then moved on in search of beaver."

"Thanks for the information," Nate said.

Touch the Clouds had stopped by the cabin and bent down to give Evelyn a final embrace before departing.

Evelyn was trying her best not to break down and bawl. She had stemmed the flow of tears, but they threatened to flow anew if she wasn't careful. Now, her doll's head in her right hand, she reached up to hug Touch the Clouds. Suddenly, her inner dam broke. She started to cry, and much to her consternation, she could not stop.

Touch the Clouds seemed as surprised as she was. He held her as gently as he might a fragile flower and glanced at Winona, who quickly came over and put an arm around her daughter's shoulder. "What is it, dear? You will see him again."

"It's not that, it's this," Evelyn said between sobs, and showed the doll's head. She felt childish, but the doll had meant so much to her.

"This would not have happened if you lived

among your own kind," Touch the Clouds said to Winona. "Our village is always well guarded."

Back when Winona took Nate as her mate and announced her intention of going to live with him in his uncle's wooden lodge, as her people called it, some of her family and many of her friends had advised against it. There was strength in numbers, they said. It was unwise to live by themselves and make it that much easier for enemies to slay them. An aunt brought up another objection: "What about the children you will have? Would you deprive them of playing with other children? Of learning their place among their own kind?"

Winona had gone off anyway, and ever since, she had been the brunt of occasional remarks that hinted all was not forgiven. To have her cousin take her to task was especially hurtful, since she cared for him so much. "We have been through this many times."

"And always your ears are plugged with wax."

If there was one thing Winona could not abide, it was having others tell her how she should live. She had always been headstrong, yet a more dutiful child never lived. Never once had she given her parents cause to think poorly of her. They had balked at her choice of a mate, too, but they had let Nate court her according to Shoshone custom, and had come to adore him almost as much as she did. "Thank you for all you have done, Cousin."

A slow smile spread across Touch the Clouds's face. "I know a hint when I hear one, as your husband would say." He pecked her on the forehead, gave Evelyn a final touch on the arm, and reined to the north. "Be well. Our people should be on the Green River for the next moon."

"Where the river bends, near where the whites used to hold their rendezvous?" Winona asked.

"That is the spot." Touch the Clouds raised a hand. Presently, the forest swallowed him and the hoofbeats of his warhorse faded.

Zach was sorry to see the warrior go. Touch the Clouds was more than kin, he was one of the few genuine friends Zach had. Unlike some Shoshones and many whites, Touch the Clouds never thought less of Zach because he was half-and-half. To the contrary, Touch the Clouds always treated him with respect, a rare commodity for a half-breed.

"We should be going, too," Louisa said. She was eager to reach their cabin and take stock of the damage. In her heart of hearts she prayed Chases Rabbits had been lying, but in her heart of hearts she knew he told the truth.

Nate came up on them without being noticed. "I have a favor to ask of the two of you," he said. They listened intently, and when he was done, they did not look thrilled.

"You want us to stay with Mother and Evelyn while you are off searching for the valley Shakespeare told you about?" Zach summed up the request. "Usually I would not object, Father, but it has been months since we saw our home."

"Besides," Lou added, "I'm not so sure moving is

something Zach and I want to do. I like it where we are."

"All I ask is that you think it over," Nate said. "Give me your answer when I get back." He put a hand on her shoulder and his other hand on Zach's. "I'm asking a lot of you. I know. But I'll be back in ten days. Two weeks at the most. And I'll rest easier knowing you're here to help Winona should she need it."

"You're worried about Rabid Wolf's bunch," Zach said. In a way, he would like it if the renegade came back. He would very much like to be the one who sent Rabid Wolf to the other side. "All right. We will stay two weeks."

"What?" Lou said.

"Two weeks, no more," Zach assured her. "If he's not back by then, we leave anyway."

"I give you my word," Nate said. Now all he had to do was break the news to Winona. Plastering a smile on his face, he walked over to where she was vainly trying to prop the front door up. "Are you in a good mood?"

Winona's glance was molten. "Of course I am in a good mood. Why would I not be, husband, with our cabin a shambles and every possession we cherished gone? Why would I not be, with hostiles out for our blood? And a fresh arrow wound in my arm?" She paused. "Why did you ask?"

"It can wait until after supper," Nate King said.

Chapter Five

It was marvelous. It was wonderful. It was everything he loved about living in the wilds.

Nate King reined up on the crest of a sawtooth ridge northwest of his valley and breathed deep of the crisp rarefied mountain air. He had forgotten how much he liked exploring new territory. Forgotten the thrill. Forgotten what it was like to be on his own. A tingle of excitement shot through him clear down to his toes.

Shifting in the saddle, Nate saw the lake near his cabin and, just visible amid the treetops, the chimney. Tendrils of smoke rose from the breakfast his wife was making for Evelyn and their guests. Zach and Louisa were staying on, as Zach promised, but Shakespeare and Blue Water Woman were bound for their cabin later that day.

A twinge of guilt smothered Nate's excitement. He always felt guilty when he left for any length of time. He couldn't help it. He was devoted to his family above all else, and all too aware of the many dangers they might face in his absence.

Still, there was no denying Nate was happy to be on his own. Just him and the bay and the sky and the woods and a myriad of wildlife and the mountains.

And two others.

Chases Rabbits and Black Beak rode slowly up toward him. The Crow was grinning. The Ute looked fit to bite the world's head off. They were astride horses that had belonged to dead members of their band, horses Zach had found grazing near the lake the evening before when he and Evelyn went to fetch water.

"You look awful happy," Nate commented as Chases Rabbits came over the rim.

"Me alive," the young Crow said.

"Only because Touch the Clouds and my son spared you yesterday," Nate reminded him. "Keep that in mind in case you get any ideas."

"You strange, Grizzly Killer," Chases Rabbits said. "Why you not kill me? Me enemy, yes?"

"Only if you want to be. I've had a few run-ins with your people over the years, but generally we get along. Several Crows are friends of mine."

"That not answer," Chases Rabbits said.

Nate did not like being pressed. "I'm not Rabid Wolf. I don't hate someone because their skin happens to be a different shade than mine."

The young Crow's forehead creased.

"And I don't go around killing men who can't defend themselves," Nate informed him. "Whites call that murder. Only a man with yellow down his spine does such a thing."

"Me not savvy," Chases Rabbits said. "Yellow? Like sun?"

"Yellow, as in one with no courage." Nate looked him in the eyes. "Only a coward kills from ambush. Only a coward kills an unarmed man. Only a coward kills women and children."

"You mean Rabid Wolf?"

"If the moccasin fits," Nate said, and turned his attention to the Ute. He made the sign language equivalents for "question" and "shoulder," which was the same as asking, "How is your wound?"

"Why do you ask?" Black Beak rejoined. "You do not care."

"If you need more salve, tell me," Nate signed. Without the ointment Winona had provided, the Ute's wound could become infected. Few folks back east realized it, but infected wounds put more people in early graves than the arrows and bullets that made the wounds to begin with.

"Why did you let us live?" Black Beak asked. "I would rub you out if you were my captive."

"I am not you," Nate signed. He noticed that Chases Rabbits was keenly interested in their exchange. "I will only kill you if you leave me no choice."

"Whites are weak," Black Beak signed. "How you have lived as long as you have is a mystery."

"You have a lot to learn about life," Nate signed. The pity of it was, the young Ute might not live long enough to learn it.

"You talk like my father and my grandfather," Black Beak signed. "They always want me to go slow. To think. But thinking is for those with gray hairs. I want to do things now, before I am too old to do them."

"Old or young, only a fool goes around killing people who have never tried to harm him."

"It will not work," Black Beak signed.

"What?"

"I am not like this silly Crow. I will not smile and treat you as a friend when you are an enemy. I kill enemies."

Chases Rabbits raised his hands from his horse. "I am not silly," he signed.

Black Beak ignored him. "You should kill me while you can, Grizzly Killer, or I will surely kill you."

"You are welcome to try." Nate rode on, angry despite himself. He intended to keep them with him until they were well away from the valley, then let them return to their people. Part of him, though, would just as soon do as the Ute was baiting him to do, and ensure they never posed a danger to his family ever again. But that wouldn't be right. He had to keep telling himself that.

Chases Rabbits was muttering to himself.

"What did you say?" Nate asked. "I didn't quite catch it."

"Stupid Utes. Think they better than Crows. Better than anyone." The young Crow laughed.

"You find that amusing, do you?"

"Black Beak not speak white tongue. What me

say, him not savvy." Chases Rabbits chuckled, then loudly declared, "All Utes dumb. All Utes have big heads. All Utes marry own mothers." He cackled at that one.

Nate was curious. "Tell me something. How did you ever get involved with Rabid Wolf's bunch, anyhow?"

"Four moons past me find tracks. Horses with shoes. Three white men come Crow land. Me tell friends. We go find."

Nate wondered who the three whites were. The days of the trappers were long over, and the wagon trail to Oregon skirted well to the north. No white man had any business being there.

"We follow tracks. We find whites. Hunters. They after mountain buffalo."

"You're sure of that?" Nate had his doubts. Mountain buffalo were far fewer in number than their prairie kin, and a lot harder to find.

"White hunters follow sign," Chases Rabbits insisted. "Not deer, not elk, mountain buffalo."

"How does Rabid Wolf enter into this?"

"Let me tell story," Chases Rabbit said. "You find out." He cleared his throat. "We find hunters. We follow. Think maybe steal Crow horses. Maybe steal guns."

The Crows were notorious thieves. The early trappers used to have a joke to the effect that if a trapper wasn't careful, the Crows would steal his nose hairs. "Go on," Nate said.

"Hunters careful. Never leave horses. Always one man guard nighttime."

"Sounds to me like they were doing all they should," Nate remarked. It also sounded as if the three whites were experienced mountaineers and not amateurs.

"We think maybe go back. Not want whites shoot us. But third night, big surprise. We camp, talk by fire. Warriors rush from dark. Have guns, bows, lances. Many of them, few of us."

"Rabid Wolf's band," Nate stated the obvious.

"Yes. They follow us and whites, both. Crows and Utes not friends, so me think they kill us. But Rabid Wolf say no. He ask we hate whites?" Chases Rabbits fell silent.

"What did you tell him?" Nate goaded.

"Me never like whites much. Father shot by whites when try steal white horses. He live, but always limp. Never same. Not smile, not play, not same father." Sadness filled the young man's voice. "Then mother's sister out pick berries. Meet white trapper. She bring our village. Live with him. Many not like. My father hate."

"How did the trapper treat you?"

"Him nice. Give me folding knife. Teach me white tongue. Then aunt and father argue. Father want white man gone. Aunt want him stay. Father and trapper argue. They draw knives. Both die."

Nate understood now. "You saw the whole thing?"

"See father stab white man. See trapper stab father. Touch father's blood. Hear death rattle." Resentment had replaced Chases Rabbits's sorrow. "Since that day, me not like whites."

"It wasn't the trapper's fault," Nate said. "You know that, don't you? Whoever he was, from the sounds of things he treated your people and you kindly."

"Him kill one me love most."

"Your father brought it on himself. He hated whites for crippling him, yet he was shot trying to steal a horse. He started the fight with the trapper by demanding the trapper leave, and drawing his knife."

"Say no more," Chases Rabbits snapped. "Me get mad."

Nate went on anyway. "When you were younger you had an excuse to hate whites. But now that you're almost a grown man yourself, you can't hide behind that excuse any longer. You must decide how you truly feel."

"Stop," Chases Rabbits repeated.

Nate shrugged. "Suit yourself," he said, and goaded the bay to a fast walk. He rode with his body slightly shifted so he could keep one eye on his two charges at all times. They were unarmed, so they couldn't stab him in the back, but he wouldn't put it past either, particularly the Ute, to try and cave his skull in or snuff his life some other way. He would be damned if he would give them the chance.

Over an hour elapsed. Nate was climbing a series of switchbacks when Chases Rabbits brought his dun up close to the bay.

"We talk, Grizzly Killer?"

"I thought you were mad at me," Nate rejoined, then smiled. "What's on your mind?"

"Your words. Make me think. You speak straight tongue. Father cause own death."

Was this a trick? Nate wondered. Or was the young Crow sincere? "Why did it take you so long to realize that?"

"Hard admit father wrong," Chases Rabbits said. "Easier hate whites. Easier want kill them."

"Which is why you joined Rabid Wolf's band," Nate commented. "Why you let him talk you into trying to kill me and my family." He paused. "But you never said what happened to those three white men you were following."

"They dead," Chases Rabbits revealed. "Rabid Wolf lay trap. We ride ahead, hide in bushes. When whites men come, we pull from horses." His voice dropped to a whisper. "They take long time die."

"Rabid Wolf tortured them?"

The young warrior blanched. "Him do things. Things me never do. Bad things. Two whites scream long while. Beg for life. Rabid Wolf kill anyway."

"What about the third one?" Nate asked.

"Him much brave. Much strong. Not scream. Not cry. Not beg. Stand tall. Call Rabid Wolf bastard. Call Rabid Wolf son of bitch. Tell Rabid Wolf untie him so they fight. Rabid Wolf refuse."

"Did you happen to learn his name? Or those of the other two?" Whenever possible, Nate tried to get word to the relatives of those killed in the mountains. No one should die nameless and forgotten.

"They not say. Rabid Wolf not ask. Him only cut. Him only laugh. Cut, laugh. Cut, laugh." Chases Rabbits shuddered.

Then and there Nate made a decision. He couldn't say when, but he was going to make it a point to hunt Rabid Wolf down and give the bigot a taste of his own bloodthirsty medicine. The world was enough of a mess without cancers like Rabid Wolf running around making things worse.

Chases Rabbits had more to say. "Me sorry try hurt you. Sorry try hurt family. Give you word never try again."

Nate wanted to believe him. He truly did. But harsh experience had taught him never to be too trusting. Of anyone. He remembered the time he brought two half-starved New Yorkers into his cabin and they repaid his kindness by trying to murder his family. Similar incidents occurred over the years. So now he never trusted anyone until they proved they deserved to be trusted. Aloud, he said, "I thank you."

"We friends now?"

"No."

"We must ride more with you?"

"Yes."

"You have hard heart, Grizzly Killer."

Nate sometimes wished that were true. Things would be a lot easier if he were more inclined to shoot first and find out why he should have shot later. He had never been quick to judge, never quick on the trigger. He always extended the benefit of the doubt, and in the process stuck his neck out to be chopped off.

But then, Nate wasn't a killer. He would blow out another's wick when he had to, when he was left with no other recourse, but by and large he believed that human life, indeed, any life whatsoever, should never be taken lightly.

Nate knew a lot of men who thought differently, including his own son. Zach would as soon shoot anyone who looked at him crosswise. Nate never could quite comprehend where his son got that from. Winona was as peaceable a soul as ever lived. Oh, she would fight to defend her brood, but neither she nor he was as prone as their oldest to blow out the wicks of others.

Strange, Nate reflected, how children could be so unlike their parents. How both parents could be loving and kind and patient, yet raise a son whose temper was forever getting him into trouble. How did that happen? Where did a person's traits come from? Zach certainly didn't take after him or Winona all that much. Nor did Zach take after his grandparents. Life was a mystery sometimes. "I wish I understood it better," Nate said aloud.

"Sorry?" Chases Rabbits said.

"Nothing." Nate grew warm in the face. He had formed the habit of talking to himself when he was alone, and on long journeys would sometimes prattle on for minutes on end. Shakespeare claimed it was normal, but Shakespeare claimed talking to his mare was normal, too. "Pay it no mind."

By the middle of the afternoon, they had passed through the ring of mountains hemming Nate's valley and were in tall timber, climbing steadily toward a pass that would take them into the next range. Nate had been this way before and was familiar with the landmarks. When a craggy bluff that slightly resembled the profile of an old man appeared, he made straight for a spring at its base.

"We'll rest the horses," Nate announced when they arrived, and conveyed the same command in sign language for Black Beak's benefit. The Ute had not signed a word in hours and was as sour as a barrel of rotten apples.

"How long you keep us?" Chases Rabbits wanted to know.

"As long as I need to." Nate figured three days should be enough. Then he would free them to return to their villages. Careful not to turn his back on them, he hunkered, dipped a hand in the cool water, and sipped from his palm.

Black Beak deliberately walked to the other side of the spring and sat with his back to them. Among some tribes it was a snub of the worst sort.

By contrast, Chases Rabbits squatted close to Nate and chuckled. "He mad at us. Hate us both, me think."

"A friend of mine likes to say that some people are born with too much acid in their systems," Nate mentioned.

"Acid?"

Nate had to remind himself that while the young Crow knew enough English to get by, he was largely ignorant of white customs and figures of speech. "It means they are born angry at the world and stay that way their whole lives."

Chases Rabbits grinned. "Black Beak, Rabid Wolf, same, same, eh?"

Nodding, Nate sipped more water, then wiped his hand on his leggings. "Isn't this better than trying to kill me?"

The question seemed to give the young Crow pause. He was thoughtful awhile, then he asked, "Grizzly Killer, all right ask something?"

"Ask whatever you want. Whether I answer depends on how personal it is."

"How many whites there be?"

Of all the questions the Crow could have come up with, Nate never expected that one. "More than there are blades of grass on the prairie."

Chases Rabbits shook his head in disbelief. "Hankton say same. Cannot be true."

"Hankton? Is that the name of the white man your aunt took up with?" Nate vaguely recollected meeting a trapper by that name many years ago at a rendezvous. From South Carolina, if he recalled correctly.

"Yes. Him have other name me not remember." Chases Rabbits studied Nate. "How there be that many? Where they all live? How they all eat?"

The young warrior was not the first Indian Nate had met who was skeptical. After all, most tribes numbered only a few thousand. Several had from five to ten thousand. A handful had over ten thousand. To them, the idea of *millions* of people was inconceivable. Nate thought the same about buffalo once. Before he came west, he heard tales of herds so huge, it took days for them to pass by. Herds that blackened the plains for miles and miles. He refused to believe it until he saw those herds with his own eyes, and learned not to scoff at such stories out of hand.

"A lot of whites live in what we call towns and cities," Nate slowly began, "which are like villages only many times bigger, and the lodges are made of stone and wood, like mine. Many more whites live in the country, on what we call farms. Farmers raise the food that feeds those who live in the towns and cities."

"Me still not savvy," Chases Rabbits said. "How can be so many?"

Nate wasn't explaining it well. He pondered, then asked, "How many babies are born to your people each year?"

"In my band? Or all Crows?"

"The entire Crow nation. Take your best guess."

Chases Rabbits gnawed on his lower lip. "In my village, twenty babies, maybe thirty. Crow nation, maybe ten times ten. Maybe less." He gestured in exasperation. "Me not sure."

"You don't need to be exact. My point is that the whites who live east of the Great Muddy River give birth to more babies each year than there are Crows in the whole Crow nation." Of which, to Nate's best reckoning, there were upward of two thousand souls. The Shoshones, on the other hand, numbered close to five thousand.

Chases Rabbits was amazed. "This can be? That many babies? You speak straight tongue?"

"I speak with a straight tongue," Nate assured him. "In the city where I was born, New York, there are over five hundred thousand whites, and that is just one city of many."

The young Crow sat back, his eyes as wide as walnuts. "Just one of many?"

Nate tried to recall some of what he had heard on his last visit east. "In another city, called Boston, there are more than one hundred and twenty thousand whites. Philadelphia has a hundred and twenty thousand. In Cincinnati, Boston, and New Orleans, there are a hundred thousand or better."

"So many!" Chases Rabbits exclaimed.

"And more all the time. Many come from other lands. From a place called Europe. And England. And Africa. Great canoes bring them by the thousands each year."

"Why?" Chases Rabbits asked.

"Why what?"

"Why whites do this? Why want so many?"

"It is the nature of my people. We breed like buffalo, and like buffalo, we are a restless breed. We are always on the go, always looking for new land to settle, or to see what is over the next horizon."

"Rabid Wolf say whites be like locusts. Say whites swarm over land, fill land with whites," Chases Rabbits said. "Him say whites kill game like killed beaver. Now few beaver left. Him say whites kill Indians until few Indians left."

"My people don't want to wipe out all Indians,"

Nate said, but even as he did, he knew it was a lie, because there *were* whites who wanted to do just that. Many whites, as a matter of fact. Maybe most.

"Want or not, them do it," Chases Rabbits said. "If many whites come, they take all land. Soon no place for my people. No place for Utes. For Sioux. For Cheyenne, Arapaho."

"It won't come to that," Nate said. But the horror of it was, it just might. Every tribe in the East had either been exterminated or forced to live where they did not want to live. There was constant talk in the newspapers and among politicians of driving *every* Indian still east of the Mississippi, west of it. A few years back, no less a personage than Davy Crockett had spoken out against it in Congress and been voted out of office. Crockett promptly announced his constituents could go to hell and he would go to Texas. He did, and met his end at the Alamo.

"My people die out like Mandans," Chases Rabbits said forlornly.

"That was different," Nate said. But was it? Once a powerful tribe that reigned supreme over the upper Missouri River, the Mandans were wiped out by a disease brought by white men: smallpox. It was said that white diseases had killed more Indians than all the bullets ever made.

"Me very sad, Grizzly Killer." Chases Rabbits was a portrait of despair. "No hope for my people."

"Nonsense," Nate said. "Some tribes live at peace with the whites, on reservations. Others, like the Wyandot Indians, have taken up white ways.

They live in white lodges and wear white clothes and send their children to white schools."

"Then they not Indians. They white."

Nate did not know what to say to that.

"Me think—" Chases Rabbits began. Suddenly, he stiffened and cried out, "Behind you! Danger, Grizzly Killer! Danger!"

Chapter Six

Nate had made a greenhorn mistake. He had let himself be distracted. He had become so caught up in his conversation with Chases Rabbits that he had forgotten about Black Beak. And the Ute was the one who would gladly slit his throat as soon as look at him.

At the young Crow's yell, Nate instinctively ducked and threw himself to the left. A searing pain lanced his right shoulder and he felt a moist, sticky sensation. He had been struck, although he did not know by what until he rolled onto his back and clawed for a pistol. His Hawken was propped on a boulder by the spring, where he had stupidly placed it.

Above him loomed Black Beak. The Ute's face was a contorted mask of consuming hatred.

Nate realized he had made yet another mistake; he had not bound their wrists before setting out that morning. He should have, but he wanted their hands free so they could handle the reins to their mounts.

Black Beak was holding a large jagged rock overhead, its surface spattered with drops of Nate's blood. "Die!" he hissed in Ute, and brought it sweeping down.

Rolling, Nate heard it thud beside him. Black Beak struck again, and missed again. Chases Rabbits shouted something, but Nate did not quite catch what it was. He had a more pressing concern: staying alive.

Black Beak sheared the jagged rock at Nate's throat. Twisting violently to one side, Nate swung a balled fist, striking the Ute's wrists. The rock missed, but not by much.

Then Nate was surging to his knees and the flintlock was out and he was thumbing back the hammer. He was going to shoot the Ute dead, dead, dead.

Black Beak's leg flicked out. His foot slammed into the pistol and sent the flintlock flying from Nate's fingers. Before Nate could draw his other flintlock, Black Beak screeched like an enraged mountain lion and swept the blood-spattered rock at Nate's skull.

Nate wasn't wearing his thick beaver hat. He had stopped using it. After years of heavy wear, in Winona's words, it looked "like something a bull buffalo dragged home after stomping it to death." If the blow landed, he was done for.

With lightning speed, Nate whipped his arms

aloft and caught hold of Black Beak's wrists. For tense seconds they struggled, the Ute red-faced and hissing, Nate grim and determined. Size and strength won out. With a powerful shove, Nate threw the younger man from him. As he did, he stuck his right foot out so that Black Beak tripped. The Ute fell to his knees.

Nate landed a punch to the jaw. He put all his weight into the swing and had the satisfaction of seeing Black Beak stretched out on his back, senseless. His hand stinging, Nate scooped up the jagged rock and stood. He was tempted, so very tempted, to do to the Ute as the Ute almost did to him. Instead, he swore and hurled the rock with all his might.

Chases Rabbits had not budged. He was staring, dumbfounded, at Black Beak.

"Thanks for your help," Nate said breathlessly. But that was unfair. The Crow's shout had saved his life.

"What I do?" Chases Rabbits asked.

"Thanks for warning me," Nate made amends. "If you hadn't yelled when you did, he would have bashed my brains out."

"Yes," the young Crow said.

"Don't sound so happy about it," Nate said sarcastically. "Maybe next time he'll be luckier."

"Me just not sure," Chases Rabbits said. He did not elaborate.

"Of what? Whether I'm your enemy or not? I spared your life, didn't I? That should tell you something right there."

"You good man, Grizzly Killer," the Crow conceded. "But you white. Your kind kill many Indians. Take much Indian land."

"Here we go again. So you hold that against me personally, do you?" Nate objected. "It's not what a man's people do that counts, it's what the man does. If every other white man on earth went out tomorrow and killed an Indian, I wouldn't take part. To me, Indians are as human as whites, and deserve to be treated the same." He had said more than he meant to, but Chases Rabbits had struck an emotional nerve. Retrieving his flintlock, he cocked it, bent over Black Beak, and smacked him. Not once but several times—hard, too, so hard his palm smarted.

The Ute groaned and his eyelids fluttered, but he did not come around.

"Grizzly Killer?" Chases Rabbits said softly.

Not wanting to take his eyes off Black Beak, Nate responded testily without looking up, "What is it?"

"You make head hurt."

Despite himself, Nate glanced at the Crow. "What on earth are you talking about? I didn't hit you."

"Make head hurt with words," Chases Rabbits clarified. "Things you say. They make me think. Make head hurt."

"Suffer in silence awhile." Nate thought the Crow would take the hint, and bent over the Ute.

"You not like other whites. You different. You better."

"I'm no better or worse than anyone else," Nate disagreed. He could mention a dozen whites who believed the same way he did. Bridger, Meek, Walker, Carson, McNair, they treated Indians as people, not as animals. Some had Indian wives. "Don't make me out to be more than I am."

The young Crow did not know when to stop flapping his gums. "Me not stupid. Most whites kill Indians when can. You not kill."

"Now is not the time for this." Nate gripped Black Beak's chin and went to shake it.

"We be friends?" Chases Rabbits asked. "Me like be friend. Like very much."

"If I let you be my friend, will you stop yapping?"

"Yapping mean talk? Then yes."

"Good. We're friends now." Nate thought the matter settled, but to his amazement, Chases Rabbits scrambled over, gripped his other hand, and pumped it with enthusiasm.

"Thank you, Grizzly Killer! You not be sorry! You see! Chases Rabbits make good friend!"

Nate stared at him, not saying a thing, until the young warrior sheepishly let go and slid back.

"Sorry. Me much excited. Me like you, Grizzly Killer. Like be your friend. Like talk with you. Like—"

"Chases Rabbits?" Nate said.

"Yes, Grizzly Killer?"

"If you don't shut up, I'll bean *you* with a rock."

The Crow laughed. "Grizzly Killer great kidder."

Black Beak groaned and stirred. Nate slapped him, then stepped back and leveled the flintlock. Almost immediately, the Ute's dark eyes opened and focused balefully on his.

"Kill me, white dog, and be done," Black Beak signed.

Nate moved farther back and sat on a boulder. Setting the pistol in his lap, he signed, "I should put a bullet between your eyes. But I told you before. I do not kill unarmed men."

"You are foolish."

"I am the one with the guns." Nate patted the pistol. "But do not let that stop you. You can try again if you want. Pick up a rock, any rock, and come at me."

"You would shoot me before I reached you," Black Beak signed.

"So? Or do you only attack whites when our backs are turned? Or from ambush?" Nate signed.

The Ute colored a furious red. "I will remember your insults."

"Remember them naked."

Black Beak tilted his head as if unsure whether he had seen the hand signs he had seen. His own hands formed the signs for "Question. Naked?"

"Take off your buckskins," Nate directed. His wound was throbbing. His shirt had been ripped, his flesh gashed. Blood trickled down his chest and back.

The Ute made no move to do as he had been told. "Are you touched in the head? I will not undress."

"Yes, you will," Nate signed, and suddenly rising, he took a long step and kicked Black Beak in the groin.

Black Beak had no chance to protect himself.

Doubling over, gasping and sputtering, he covered himself and groaned.

"Do that again!" Chases Rabbits said. "Him call me silly."

Nate folded his arms and waited. At length, the gasps and the sputters ended and Black Beak wiped a sleeve across his mouth and slowly sat up.

"I will kill you for that."

"Only if I turn my back," Nate signed. "Now take off your buckskins and your moccasins."

Black Beak hesitated. "This is no way to treat an enemy."

"Would you rather I sneak up behind you and hit you with a rock?" Nate's patience was at an end.

Black Beak glanced at Chases Rabbits, who laughed, then began removing his moccasins, first one and then the other. He placed them neatly beside him and started sliding his shirt off.

"Too slow," Nate signed. The whole right side of his chest was damp.

Black Beak's shirt joined his moccasins. He lowered his hands to his waist but stopped. "Let this be enough."

Nate made as if to kick him, and Black Beak quickly shed his last article of clothing.

The Ute sat with his knees bent and his arms over his manhood, glowering. "Why did you have me do this? So I will not try to kill you again? I do not need clothes to do that."

"Thank you for reminding me," Nate signed, and brought his right heel crashing down on Black Beak's left foot. There was a sharp *crack,* and Black

Beak howled and clutched his toes and thrashed back and forth.

"Me break other foot?" Chases Rabbits eagerly requested.

"One is enough," Nate said. He had only broken a toe or two. Or possibly three. He waited until the fit subsided and Black Beak was lying on his side, grimacing and wheezing. "You can go now," he signed.

Black Beak's hatred was practically a physical force. He did not want to let go of his foot, but he did to ask, "What?"

"You are free to go to your village. Without weapons and clothes, it will take you many sleeps. But you can make it if you are careful."

"Go like this?" Black Beak was shaking, but not from the pain. He was shaking in pure rage.

"It is how you came into the world," Nate signed.

"What if a bear finds me? Or I meet a blood war party or other enemies?" Black Beak gnashed his teeth and clenched and unclenched his hands, as if he yearned to have them wrapped around Nate's throat.

"Limp fast," Nate advised.

"I want to kill you so much." Black Beak got his good leg under him and began to crawl toward the trees.

"Hold up," Nate said, and when the Ute looked quizzically up, he touched the hilt of his Bowie. "Stay away from me and my family. The next time I see you, it will be me or you."

"You are foolish," Black Beak reiterated. He resumed crawling. The woods were not that far. He came to the tree line and picked up a downed limb. Removing the leaves and offshoots, he propped the limb under him and carefully stood. Then, bestowing a last glare in Nate's direction, he hobbled into the vegetation and was gone.

Chases Rabbits exploded in mirth and slapped his thigh. "You clever, Grizzly Killer!"

Nate was gingerly stripping off his own shirt. His shoulder still hurt like hell. "Think so?"

"Me know so. Me know why you make him undress. Know why you break his toes."

"Do you?" Nate absently said while examining the wound. The gash was a good four inches long and a quarter of an inch deep. The bleeding had almost stopped, but he had lost a lot of blood. His shirt and his torso were stained red. It explained why he felt somewhat light-headed.

"Yes, me do," Chases Rabbits was saying. "You not want Black Beak hurt your family. You make sure he not go back your valley."

That was the general idea, Nate mentally agreed, but he took no particular glee in what he had done. Naked, unarmed, and with a bad foot, Black Beak would think of one thing and one thing only: reaching his people as rapidly as he could.

"Very clever." Chases Rabbits grinned. "Take Black Beak whole moon reach Ute village. Next moon for foot heal. You be home then. Protect family."

"You have it all figured out," Nate said as he

moved to the spring and hunkered. "Now figure out what I should do with you."

Chases Rabbits stopped smiling. "No need take clothes. No need break toes. Me friend now. Me not try kill you."

Bending, Nate dipped his hand in the spring and splashed water on his shoulder, chest, and back. Goose bumps prickled his skin. It took a while to wash away all the blood. When he was done, he sat on a boulder.

"What you do, Grizzly Killer?" Chases Rabbits asked.

"I'm waiting to dry off, then I'll apply some salve and rig a bandage," Nate explained.

"Not that," Chases Rabbits said. "What we do here? Where we go?"

"I'm on a quest." That was all Nate would reveal. He was not completely convinced the young Crow could be trusted.

"What is 'quest'? Me not remember word."

"A quest is a hunt," Nate said.

"What kind this hunt be? No animal called quest me know of. No place called quest, like whites call Eagle Mountain Long's Peak."

Nate figured an explanation would shut him up. "When a man is searching for something, whites say he is on a quest. There is a story my people are fond of that took place long ago, about a hero who went on a quest to find the Golden Fleece."

"What that be?"

Nate did not care to relate the entire story of Jason and the Argonauts. He had only mentioned it to make his point. "The Golden Fleece was a ram's skin."

"What be ram?"

"It's like the male mountain sheep your people sometimes hunt high on the cliffs," Nate clarified. "Only, the hide of this one was made of gold."

"Gold? The yellow rocks whites love?" Chases Rabbits scratched his head. "How ram have rock skin?"

Nate was sorry he had brought it up. "It's a story. A myth." He could tell the Crow was completely confused. "A tale of ancient times, long before whites came across the great water to this land. When the world was young."

Chases Rabbits nodded vigorously. "Me savvy now. Absorake call Old Times. When Old Man made world."

The Absorake, Nate knew, was what the Crows called themselves. Although he had heard a few refer to themselves as Apsaruke. Either way, it was the name of a bird that no longer existed. But just as the Sosoni hand sign for their tribe, a wavy movement reminiscent of a crawling serpent, had resulted in whites calling the Sosonis "Snakes," so, too, had the early hand sign for the Absorake, which was the same for "bird," resulted in their tribe being commonly called "Crows."

"You know Old Man?" Chases Rabbits asked.

Nate nodded. Crow legend had it that at one time the only beings in existence were Old Man and four ducks. One day Old Man had one of the ducks dive to the bottom of the sea and bring up some dirt in its beak. Old Man then blew on the dirt, and the mountains and the plains came to be. He blew on the dirt again, and the first people appeared, an Absorake man and woman.

It was of special interest to Nate that according to the Crow legend, the first couple were blind. When Old Man opened their eyes, they saw that they were naked. Old Man showed them how to kill and skin a buffalo so they would have something to wear.

"What quest Grizzly Killer on?" Chases Rabbits would not let it drop.

"I'm looking for someone who doesn't pester me with endless questions," Nate responded irritably.

Chases Rabbits cackled. "Grizzly Killer funny. What you really look for? Why you not say?"

"It's personal," Nate said.

"But why you not say?" Chases Rabbits was fidgeting from excess curiosity. "It be big secret? Is that it?" He gazed eastward, in the direction they had come, then to the northwest, in the direction they were headed. "What out there interest you?"

"Maybe I'll tell you later," Nate said to forestall more probing, and to his relief, Chases Rabbits stopped quizzing him. He went about taking a beaded parfleche off his bay and applying salve to his wound.

Suddenly, the young Crow's face materialized above his shoulder. Nate gave a start and stabbed his left hand to a pistol. "What in God's name are you up to? Don't sneak up on me like that."

"Sorry. You bad hurt. Need fix." Chases Rabbits made a sewing motion with his hands.

"I'm fine," Nate said in annoyance. Winona would want to sew it up, too, if she were there, but then, she always was a mother hen.

Chases Rabbits wagged a finger at him. "Grizzly Killer scared me hurt him?"

"No," Nate snapped.

"Then me sew for you."

"No."

"Me fix good."

"No."

"You have needle? Thread?"

As a matter of fact, Nate did, but he was not about to admit it. He always brought a sewing kit in case his buckskins needed mending. "Go jump in the spring."

Chases Rabbits glanced at the pool. "Why me want do that?" He sniffed at an armpit. "Me smell?"

"Better yet, climb the bluff and jump off."

The young Crow craned his neck back and stared at the rim sixty feet above them. "Grizzly Killer poke fun? That right, yes? That what whites say?"

From the same parfleche, Nate removed a roll of brown cloth. Once it had been part of an old towel Winona cut into strips for bandages. Unrolling it, he clamped one end under his arm and wrapped it around and around his shoulder. It kept slipping, because he couldn't reach back far enough.

"Let me," Chases Rabbits volunteered, and snatched the bandage from Nate's grasp. "Me do good."

Nate felt uncomfortable having him so close.

Without being obvious, he rested his hand on the Bowie. "Go ahead if you want."

Chases Rabbits beamed like a youngster who had just been given his first pony. "Grizzly Killer trusts me!"

No, Nate didn't, but the young Crow was so consarned likable, Nate felt a tweak of conscience. "Just do it."

"Sew cut first," Chases Rabbits said, and began unraveling what Nate had done. "Must do right or not do."

To argue would only result in another round of squabbling. Nate handed over the sewing kit.

"What this?" Chases Rabbits opened the leather pouch and upended it over a flat rock. Out spilled several spools of thread and a lucifer box. Chases Rabbits had to pry at the box before he figured out to how to open it, and when he did, he opened it upside down. Out fell several metal needles, several bone needles, and a thimble. "What be this?" he marveled, holding up the latter.

"It's so you won't prick yourself," Nate explained, and showed him how the thimble fit.

Chases Rabbits held the thimble in both hands as if it were the Holy Grail. He tried it on each of his fingers, admiring how it gleamed in the sunlight. Then he stuck it on his right thumb and couldn't get it off. A look of panic seized him. "Help, Grizzly Killer!"

"You big baby." Nate dipped the Crow's hand in the spring, pulled it out, and easily slid the thimble off.

"Thank you! Me worried not come off."

"Too bad it can't fit over your mouth."

"Sorry?"

"Just get this over with."

But Chases Rabbits had to examine every one of the needles. The bone needles were not of much interest since they were similar to those his own people used, but the metal needles fascinated him no end. He tested each one by jabbing himself in the palm. "Mother like these plenty."

"Let's get this over with sometime this year."

"Year?" Chases Rabbits said, and tittered. "You very funny, Grizzly Killer. Me tell you that yet?"

"Twice now," Nate said, and was puzzled when a shadow fell across them. He thought that maybe a stray cloud was blocking out the sun, and glanced skyward. But it wasn't a cloud. It was a boulder. Plummeting right down on top of them.

Chapter Seven

There are some sights so unexpectedly shocking that they freeze the beholder in bewilderment. Nate King was stunned by the sight of the boulder falling from atop the bluff. For a precious second he was frozen in place. Then he bellowed, "Look out!" and threw himself to one side, looping an arm around Chases Rabbits as he leaped and bearing the young Crow with him.

The crash of the impact was as loud as a thunderclap. Nate lay on his belly, the sound ringing in his ears, as a thick cloud of dust enveloped him. Without thinking, he inhaled and broke into a fit of coughing. Twisting, he saw that the boulder had missed them by less than two feet.

Chases Rabbits inhaled even more of the dust and was hacking and blinking. He shouted something in the Crow tongue and pointed upward.

One look turned the ice in Nate's veins into fire.

Silhouetted against the sky at the very edge of the bluff was a naked figure with a long, thick tree branch in his hand. One end of the branch was wedged under a large boulder that Black Beak, his face flushed and his chest heaving, was straining mightily to dislodge and send hurtling down on top of them. He was looking down at them, his hatred evident even at that distance, a budding smirk of triumph on his face.

The boulder had begun to move.

Nate glanced around for his Hawken. He had neglected to grab it when he leaped. Shifting, he beheld its shattered stock jutting from under the first boulder. His rifle had been crushed.

In the wilderness, a white man without a rifle was a man living on borrowed time. It was an indispensable tool, even more essential than a pistol or a knife in that a rifle lent the advantage of range and penetration, advantages crucial in a clash with a grizzly or a band of hostiles.

Or when a revenge-crazed warrior was trying to push a massive boulder down on one's head.

Nate streaked his hands to his waist. He drew both flintlocks simultaneously, cocking them as he elevated his arms. Black Beak saw him draw them but did not let go of the branch and dive for cover. The Ute sneered, as if daring Nate to try and shoot him.

Nate obliged. At the *crack,* his right flintlock belched smoke and lead. Up on the rim, Black Beak reacted as if he had been punched in the ribs. But he still did not release the branch. Bent half over, blood trickling from a corner of his mouth, he put all he had into tumbling the boulder from its roost. Another few moments and it would hurtle over the edge.

Nate took aim. Holding the heavy pistol steady, he sucked in a breath, then smoothly stroked the trigger.

Black Beak's face dissolved and the top of his head exploded in a shower of hair, bone, and flesh. He staggered, his hands opening spasmodically, and the branch he had been using as a crutch slipped from his grasp. His arms started to rise, but all brain function had ceased and they fell limp even as he did the same. His body took a final step, and over the brink he came, the limb he had been using falling with him.

Heaving erect, Nate shouted, "Move!" and jumped out of the way.

Yelping, Chases Rabbits scrambled on all fours like an oversized crab, slipping twice before he gained speed.

The thud of the body was nowhere near as loud as the crash of the boulder, and was punctuated by the clatter of the branch.

Nate slowly uncurled and turned. He expected it to be grisly, and it was. His stomach churned, but only briefly.

Black Beak had hit face first. His head had split like an overripe melon and his brains had burst out. What little was left of his features was barely recognizable as human. One of his eyeballs had popped from its socket and lay at arm's length from the body. His neck was a blood-smeared stump. A broken shoulder bone had ruptured through his skin, the bone gleaming white in the sunshine.

Chases Rabbits breathed a few words in Crow, then switched to English. "Him very dead."

"Good riddance," Nate said. The young Ute should have left while he had the chance instead of sneaking back and scaling the bluff. There had to be a trail to the top somewhere, probably to the south, where a gradual slope led to the summit.

"Him want me dead too," Chases Rabbits said, visibly shaken. "Never trust Utes. Them bad medicine."

The Utes generally felt the same about the Crows, Nate recalled, but he did not remind Chases Rabbits. "He's no great loss. But that rifle is."

"What you do now? Need long gun, yes?"

"Yes," Nate said. Could he get by without one? Moving well back from the blood and gore, he went to sit so he could reload his pistols. A whinny brought him up short.

Their horses were racing away through the trees. The smell of fresh blood had been too much for nerves frayed by the crash of the boulder, and even Nate's usually dependable bay was running off. "Damn!" he fumed, and took off after them. He had gone only a few yards when Chases Rabbits appeared at his elbow.

"Stupid horses. Important we catch."

"Very important," Nate huffed. Losing the rifle was bad enough. Losing the horses would be a calamity. He would have no recourse but to turn back, and it would take five times as long to reach his cabin on foot as it would on horseback. Days and nights of being at the mercy of the elements and anyone and anything inclined to do him harm.

The horses disappeared in the distance, but Nate did not slow or stop. Their panic would fade and they would halt after a while to graze. They would be tired and easy to catch.

"Me want thank you, Grizzly Killer," Chases Rabbits said. "You save me."

"You did the same for me earlier," Nate responded.

They ran in silence awhile, then Chases Rabbits asked, "Why all whites not like you?"

"No two people are ever the same," Nate said absently. He was trying to spot the horses.

"You not like other whites. You nice."

Nate was flattered by the compliment, but said, "There are a lot of nice whites. Just as there are a lot of nice Crows and nice Utes."

"Utes too?" Chases Rabbits was skeptical. "Next you say there be nice Apaches." He laughed at his little joke.

"People are people," Nate remarked. It didn't matter if they were red or white, there were good ones and bad ones. There were those who were kindly and those who were not. Those who offered their hand in friendship to one and all and those who would gladly stab one and all in the back.

"My people special," Chases Rabbits said. "Your people special you?"

Nate had never been one of those who thought his kind had a monopoly on the best aspects of human nature. Nor did he subscribe to the belief that other races were inferior simply because they were different. "There is special, and there is special," he replied.

"Me not savvy."

"Remind me some other time and I'll explain," Nate offered. He needed all his breath for running.

"Grizzly Killer?" Chases Rabbits said.

Nate looked at him.

"Me like you, Grizzly Killer. You good man. Me sorry about before. Sorry try kill you." The boy's sincerity was evident.

"We all make mistakes." Nate knew whereof he spoke. He had made more than his share.

They were making a lot of noise since Nate was not trying to move stealthily. The important thing was to find the horses, and find them quickly. He did not think much of it when a rabbit bolted out of a thicket and bounded off in high, frantic leaps. Nor did he use more caution when several sparrows shot up into the air, chirping in alarm. He assumed Chases Rabbits and he were to blame. Then he rounded a trunk, and there, not ten feet away, was a black bear.

Nate stopped so abruptly, he nearly tripped over his own feet. The bear was tearing apart an old log to get at grubs. It must have heard them, yet it had not run off. Now it raised its head and growled an ominous warning, annoyed by the intrusion.

Nate imitated a tree. He wanted to kick himself

for going after the horses before reloading his pistols. The irony of his comment about making mistakes was not lost on him. He had just made several in unthinking succession, and all he had now to defend himself with were his Bowie and his tomahawk.

Chases Rabbits had also stopped and was trembling like an aspen leaf in a strong wind. "Big bear!" he whispered. "We run?"

"No," Nate whispered. It had been his experience that running sometimes triggered an attack. Something about a fleeing figure caused meateaters to charge even when they were not inclined to do so. The black bear was staring and sniffing. Nate prayed it wouldn't decide to dine on something considerably bigger than those grubs.

The bear was on the other side of the log. Now it raised a foreleg to step over, then stopped, another growl rumbling deep in its barrel chest.

"We run?" Chases Rabbits anxiously repeated. The whites of his eyes were showing and he was poised to bolt.

"No," Nate whispered. They had three other choices. They could back off slowly. They could stand there and wait for the bear to make up its ursine mind. Or they could do what Nate did next, which was to advance *toward* the bear while raising his arms overhead and hollering, "Ho! Bear! Go away! Leave us be!"

Chases Rabbits squeaked like a mouse. "You crazy, Grizzly Killer!"

There was a method to Nate's seeming insanity.

Experience had also taught him that most animals would back down when a man came at them making a lot of noise. The big predators, in particular, became confused when potential prey did not act like prey should. Add to that the fact that most animals were naturally wary of man. Humankind was unlike any other creatures in the wild, and the wild things knew that, and shunned humans accordingly. Maybe it was an ages-old instinct that told them humans were dangerous. Or maybe it was the strangeness humans radiated. Whatever the case, Nate was counting on his loud display to accomplish what his expended pistols could not.

The black bear growled louder than ever but did not charge.

"Go, you mangy brute!" Nate bawled. "Get out of here! Go find a she-bear to frolic with!" For all he knew, it was a she-bear. He was just saying whatever popped into his head.

Suddenly, Chases Rabbits raised his arms and began hopping up and down. "Go, stupid bear! Go play with snakes!"

Nate wondered what in the world snakes had to do with anything. "*Go!*" he roared, and took a gamble. Shrieking at the top of his lungs, he rushed forward.

The bear didn't move. For harrowing moments the outcome hung in a feral balance, then the black bear grunted and swung around and briskly lumbered off into the woods.

Chases Rabbits yipped for joy. "We scare him, Grizzly Killer!"

"Don't count on it," Nate said. Bears were known to circle back now and then. He kept on yelling for more than a minute, until he was satisfied it was truly gone.

"You like shout?" the young Crow asked.

Nate sat on what was left of the log and commenced reloading. The pistols would not stop a grizzly, but they might cripple or kill a black bear if he put a slug in the right place.

Chases Rabbits slapped his leg. "Wait me tell friends! Run off bear! Plenty brave, eh?"

"Plenty lucky," Nate said as he opened his powder horn. In the end, things always boiled down to luck in a clash between a man and a living engine of destruction like a bear.

"Me chase baby bear once," Chases Rabbits mentioned. "Make mother bear angry, so me run."

Nate asked something that had been on his mind for some time. "Tell me. How did you ever get a name like Chases Rabbits?"

"When me little, rabbit come in village. Me see. Me try catch."

"But you're old enough now that you can choose a new name if you want, can't you?"

"Me like Chases Rabbits. Makes people think me fast."

"It takes all kinds," Nate said under his breath. He was still watching the vegetation, but the black bear had not reappeared.

Out of the blue, Chases Rabbits said, "Your daughter pretty."

"That she is," Nate agreed. Evelyn took after her

mother in that regard. "She'll grow into a beautiful woman one day."

"She have man?"

About to reach into his ammo pouch, Nate glanced up. "Don't even think it. She's much too young."

"Sisters older when warriors take them," Chases Rabbits said.

Among some tribes it was the custom for girls to marry quite young. By the age of fourteen, in some instances. "My daughter won't be ready to marry for five or six winters yet," Nate said.

The young Crow snorted. "She be old woman."

"Maybe so, but my people don't rush into wedlock. A girl can do it any age she pleases." Preferably, Nate thought, when she was a *woman*.

"Maybe me court her," Chases Rabbits said.

"Maybe me shoot you," Nate mimicked him.

"You mean that?"

"I'll hang a sign out when she is old enough and announce it to the whole world," Nate said.

"Sign?"

Nate did not explain. "There's nothing wrong with marrying young, I suppose. My people used to do it a lot more regularly than we do it these days. In some places, parents arranged marriages before their children were even born. But that's not how we do things now. We don't force women to marry whether they want to or not. They have the freedom to choose who and when."

Chases Rabbits brightened. "So Grizzly Killer's daughter marry when want?"

GET
4 FREE BOOKS!

You can have the best Westerns delivered to your door for less than what you'd pay in a bookstore or online. Sign up for one of our book clubs today, and we'll send you **4 FREE* BOOKS**, worth $23.96, just for trying it out...**with no obligation to buy, ever!**

Authors include classic writers such as
LOUIS L'AMOUR, MAX BRAND, ZANE GREY
and more; PLUS new authors such as
COTTON SMITH, TIM CHAMPLIN, JOHNNY D. BOGGS
and others.

As a book club member you also receive the following special benefits:
- **30% OFF** all orders through our website & telecenter!
- **Exclusive access to special discounts!**
- **Convenient home delivery and 10 days to return any books you don't want to keep.**

There is no minimum number of books to buy,
and you may cancel membership at any time.
See back to sign up!

*Please include $2.00 for shipping and handling.

YES! ☐

Sign me up for the Leisure Western Book Club
and send my FOUR FREE BOOKS! If I choose to stay
in the club, I will pay only $13.44* each month,
a savings of $10.52!

NAME: _____

ADDRESS: _____

_____

TELEPHONE: _____

E-MAIL: _____

☐ **I WANT TO PAY BY CREDIT CARD.**

☐ VISA   ☐ MasterCard.   ☐ DISCOVER

ACCOUNT #: _____

EXPIRATION DATE: _____

SIGNATURE: _____

Send this card along with $2.00 shipping & handling to:

**Leisure Western Book Club
20 Academy Street
Norwalk, CT 06850-4032**

Or fax (must include credit card information!) to: 610.995.9274.
You can also sign up online at www.dorchesterpub.com.

*Plus $2.00 for shipping. Offer open to residents of the U.S. and Canada only.
Canadian residents please call 1.800.481.9191 for pricing information.
If under 18, a parent or guardian must sign. Terms, prices and conditions subject to change. Subscription subject
to acceptance. Dorchester Publishing reserves the right to reject any order or cancel any subscription.

JOIN NOW!

"Sure," Nate said. "So long as I don't have any objections." It was not a subject he cared to discuss further, so he asked, "Isn't there a Crow girl you're fond of?"

"Many," Chases Rabbits said. "One called Morning Mist like most. We play when little. She grow be pretty woman."

"Girls have a habit of doing that." Nate finished reloading the first flintlock and started in on the second.

"You love Shoshone woman?"

"What a dumb question," Nate scoffed. "Of course I love her, as I've never loved anyone. She is all I could ever want in a wife, and much more. She has stood by me through good times and bad, and never let me down."

"Me want woman like that," Chases Rabbits said. "Daughters like mothers, eh?"

It took a moment for what the younger man was suggesting to sink in. "You would be better off with a Crow woman," Nate said. "Mixed marriages don't always work out." He was just saying that. Fact was, a lot of trappers had taken Indian wives and been happy ever after.

Chases Rabbits was young, but he wasn't gullible. "Yours work out," he noted.

The pistols were loaded. Nate stood, wedged them under his wide leather belt, and cast about for sign of their horses. He found where the fleeing animals had nearly blundered onto the bear and swerved to the north to avoid it. Breaking into a dogtrot, he wound through the dense timber.

The young Crow paced him.

"So we're friends now, are we?" Nate asked.

"If you want be, yes."

"Then, when we find the horses, you're free to return to your people." Nate saw no purpose to continuing to treat the boy as an enemy. He didn't consider him a threat to his family anymore.

"You want me go?" Chases Rabbits sounded disappointed.

"I should think you would be happy," Nate said. "You're welcome to the horse, too." It had belonged to a Ute.

"Me thank you."

They ran in silence, but not for long.

"Grizzly Killer, why you want me go? You no like?"

"I like you just fine," Nate said. Which was true to a point. The youth had a knack for grating on his nerves.

"Me want go with you," Chases Rabbits said. "Me want be friend."

Nate chuckled. "One day you try to kill me, the next you want to be my pard? I appreciate the change of heart. I truly do. But it's best we go our separate ways."

"Why?"

Nate glanced at him. The young warrior asked the most aggravating questions. "Because I have things to do and I can do them better alone."

"The quest you tell about?"

"Yes," Nate said, hoping that would end it. He should have known better.

"Me help on quest."

"That's kind of you, but it's personal." Nate did not want the Crow to learn where he might relocate.

"What means 'personal'?" Chases Rabbits inquired.

Nate sighed. "When something is personal, it's your business and no one else's. Private things. Things you don't want anyone else to know."

"What kind things?"

Fortunately for Nate, at that instant he spied the horses up ahead in a clearing. "Look yonder!" He hastened to reclaim them before they ran off. Covered with sweat, they were chomping grass.

The bay didn't shy when Nate took the reins. Mounting, he checked his remaining parfleche. It was intact, the contents undisturbed. The other parfleche, like his rifle, had fallen victim to the boulder. He took hold of the reins to the horse Black Beak had been riding, then jerked his thumb at the third animal. "It's all yours, Chases Rabbits, with my blessings."

The young Crow reluctantly walked over. "Me go with you while yet? How that be?"

"You can't take no for an answer," Nate said curtly. He liked the boy, but there were limits.

"Much honor be friend Grizzly Killer," Chases Rabbits said. "Me help hunt, help cook, help guard horses."

"That's nice of you," Nate said, "but here is where we part company. You're welcome to visit me if you're ever in my neck of the woods." He discreetly did not mention that his neck of the woods might soon change.

Chases Rabbits swung onto the horse and sat there, frowning. "Me really want come."

"Another time." Nate smiled and touched a finger to his forehead and reined to the northwest, leading the extra horse. He deliberately did not look back. When he had gone a hundred yards and the young Crow did not shout for him to stop or try to overtake him, he exhaled in relief and patted the bay. "At last we're on our own."

For the rest of the afternoon and into the evening, Nate enjoyed blessed peace and quiet. It was wonderful to ride along and hear only the jays and ravens and squirrels. He stopped just once, at the bluff, to see if there was any way to get at the parfleche under the boulder. There wasn't. He would have to do without Winona's healing salve until he returned to their cabin.

Which was too bad. His hurt shoulder was bothering him. He had to be careful how high he raised his arm or pain spiked through it. There was no evidence of infection, though, and that was the important thing.

Toward sundown, Nate made camp on a ridge that afforded a sweeping vista of the lower peaks and foothills. He gathered sticks and kindling, and with the help of his fire steel and flint soon had a fire crackling. Indian-fashion, he kept it small. Whites were notorious for building campfires big enough to be seen on the moon, but a large fire was a beacon to every enemy who saw it, and at night a fire could be spotted from a long ways off.

His remaining parfleche contained pemmican and jerky, enough to subsist on for a week if he had to. Several pieces sufficed for his supper. That, and water from the water skin he had filled at the spring.

Eager to be on the move at daybreak, Nate turned in early. He tried to sleep, but tossed and turned until almost midnight. Part of it had to do with being alone for the first time in such a long time. When he was in his twenties, he would go off for weeks to trap, but those days were long gone.

Part of it, too, a part Nate was ashamed to admit, was that he had grown soft. He was used to sleeping in a comfortable bed with a roof over his head. Oh, he had slept out under the stars for days on end during his recent trek east, but then he had Winona beside him to keep him warm and cozy at night. He had her warmth, her smell, her love.

Now Nate was alone, and for the first time since he came to the mountains decades ago, it did not sit well with him.

The sun had not yet risen when Nate was in the saddle and on the move. He craved his usual morning coffee but fought down the desire. The sooner he started out, the more ground he could cover, and the sooner he could be with his wife and daughter again.

A golden eye was peeking over the edge of the world when Nate drew rein on a grassy shelf, stretched, and yawned. Sunrise promised to be spectacular. A pink band laced with brilliant splashes of yellow and orange framed the sky and was growing brighter by the second.

Nate was so entranced by the vivid hues that he almost failed to spot a row of riders half a mile down the mountain. A tingle shot through him. Shielding his eyes, he watched them closely, hoping against hope they were not following him. But there could be no doubt.

They were smack on his trail.

Chapter Eight

There were several possibilities. The riders might be white, but Nate doubted it. White men that deep in the mountains were rare. The nearest outpost, Bent's Fort, was hundreds of miles away. The riders might be friendly Indians, but again, Nate was doubtful. He was on the border of Ute country, and the Utes were not on the best of terms with their neighbors, so their neighbors tended to fight shy of the area.

The likeliest possibility was that they were hostiles, and if so, then Nate had a fair notion who they were. He watched them a few minutes, long enough to confirm that they were following his tracks. Several times the lead rider bent low, plainly reading the sign.

Seven of them, and Nate without his Hawken. Facing northwest, he gigged the bay onward and upward.

Nate wasn't worried. Yet. He had a sizable lead. He had two horses and could ride them in relays, switching when one tired. He had spotted the stalkers before they spotted him, and that alone might make the difference between living and the alternative.

For the moment, Nate was content to ride hard. He made no effort to hide his tracks. Doing so would alert the riders that he was onto them and maybe spur them into overtaking him that much sooner. He must play this smart. He must not let on that he knew, and at the same time, he must lose them.

Nate was mildly surprised they had come after him. After the licking they took, he would have thought they would be halfway to their village. He was also mildly relieved that they were out to kill him and not his family. Or maybe they planned to do the latter after they had done the former.

He wouldn't make it easy for them. He had lived in the wilds for decades and knew every trick there was. The loss of his rifle was a major handicap, but he still had his pistols and his knife and tomahawk.

All morning, Nate pushed deeper into the high country. At about ten, he came to a stream and allowed both horses to drink and briefly rest. Then he was on the move again, on the sorrel and leading the bay.

Noon found him on a high shelf. While the horses grazed, Nate dropped onto his belly and scanned the slopes below. It was not long before he saw them, winding steadily upward. They were farther back, a mile or more, and not in any particular hurry. That told him they were biding their time. They planned to stick to his trail and jump him after he bedded down for the night.

Nate could fight or he could try and lose them. It was tempting to finish what he had started, but why risk having his blood spilled? Losing them would be difficult, but it could be done.

Nate entered the next stream he came to and rode upstream in the middle. The swiftly flowing water erased many of the prints, but not all. A determined tracker could still follow him. It would just take longer.

After a couple of miles, Nate reined onto the right bank and studied the terrain above the timberline. There the ground was always hard as iron, and so rocky in spots that a man, or a horse, left few tracks.

Soon Nate was above the timber and using all the skill he possessed to shake his pursuers. Avoiding softer patches of soil, he stuck to the rockiest ground. At times solid rock was under hoof. He could not avoid leaving an occasional track, but they were few and considerably far between. He grinned at the thought of how mad it would make those who were after him.

It was not uncommon for thunderstorms to develop at that altitude late in the afternoon, but today Nate had no such luck. Still, he had increased his lead enough that the seven riders were not about to catch up to him before sunset. He had gained another night, and that was his intention all along.

Nate did not waste the four remaining hours of daylight. He rode until dark. In a stand of pines high on a west slope, he tied the horses, spread out his blanket, and lay down to catch what sleep he could. It was not a lot. He was too tense, too excited. By his reckoning it was past eleven when he rose, rolled up the blanket, and tied it on the bay. Then, leaving the sorrel, he retraced his steps as best he was able in the dark.

Gusts of wind whipped Nate's hair. The wind carried with it the wavering howls of wolves and the higher-pitched yips of coyotes. Once a painter screeched, sounding like a woman in the throes of childbirth.

Nate figured his pursuers would be two or three miles back, and he was not far off the mark: They were two and a half. Since there were no trees and little brush, they had made camp in the open, and the flickering flame of their small fire served as a beacon.

When Nate was near enough that he could distinguish a figure moving about, he drew rein and dismounted. Crouching, he cat-footed closer. Six of the warriors were sleeping. They had turned in early to get an early start.

The seventh was keeping watch and he was having a hard time of it. He kept yawning and stretching, and would rise from time to time to pace back and forth or walk over to the horses.

Nate flattened and crawled. Some of the sleepers were facing him, some weren't. The visage of one who was filled his breast with cold fury.

Rabid Wolf was on his side, his hands under his head. A bow and quiver lay next to him.

Suddenly, the warrior by the fire stood up. Nate stopped crawling. Thinking he had been seen, he started to reach for a flintlock but stopped when the warrior merely arched his back and began walking back and forth in another effort to stay awake.

Nate did not have all night. He waited impatiently for the Ute to sit back down, then snaked toward their horses.

It wasn't necessary to kill them to beat them. All Nate had to do was *strand* them afoot and he would be rid of them.

The horses were tethered close together, a precaution against their being stolen or spooked. Like their owners, they were dozing. Not one raised its head or pricked its ears until Nate was only a few yards away.

Would the horses nicker and act up? Sometimes horses did, sometimes horses didn't. These didn't.

Nate slid his Bowie from its sheath. Moving slowly so as not to scare them, he cut their hobbles. They stayed where they were. They were too well trained to run off unless provoked. So he prepared to provoke them.

Nate backed slowly away until he was a good thirty feet from the camp. He groped about until he located half a dozen rocks about the size of hen's eggs. Hefting one, he threw it at a horse. The rock hit with an audible *thuck*, and the startled horse did what Nate hoped it would do. It whinnied and shied. Quickly, Nate threw the rest, one after the other. Another horse nickered. A third bolted, and when it did, the rest were swift to follow suit.

The warrior by the fire rushed to stop them, but it was too late. He snatched at the mane of the last one but could not hold on. He could only give chase. With a shout to his companions, some of whom had jumped up and were glancing around in confusion, he sprinted into the dark.

Rabid Wolf and the rest went flying on his heels. They were not fully awake, and several made the mistake of leaving their bows and lances behind.

Nate waited for the sounds of the bedlam to fade, then he warily entered the ring of firelight and picked up a bow and quiver. It was now his. Two other bows and quivers and two lances he placed on the fire. The same with a tomahawk someone had left behind.

Then Nate was hurrying to the bay. He slung the quiver across his back as he ran. Grinning, he imaged their expressions when they returned to find some of their weapons reduced to charred embers.

Mounting the bay, Nate rode at a walk until he had gone far enough that they would not hear. An hour before dawn, he was back with the sorrel. Hungrily chewing pemmican, he examined the bow. Superbly crafted from ash and fitted with a sinew string, it was powerful enough to drive an arrow clean through a man's chest. The quiver held twenty-one arrows, more than enough to see him through.

Nate was quite pleased with himself. He still had

what it took to hold his own—against enemies half his age, no less. Winona would be proud.

The morning broke crisp and clear. It did not stay cool for long. The breeze died and the temperature steadily climbed. A few pillowy clouds sprinkled the azure vault above.

Nate rode happily along, truly enjoying himself for the first time since he left his cabin. He watched a hawk soar on outstretched wings, admired the ability of a pair of mountain sheep to navigate a precipitous crag, and grinned at the antics of a chipmunk he accidentally disturbed.

Nate had never been superstitious, but perhaps his outfoxing of Rabid Wolf was an omen of things to come. Of the new life he would carve out for himself and his loved ones in a part of the Rockies solely their own.

The more Nate thought about it, the more he chided himself for staying in his uncle's cabin so long. All those years, all those clashes with the Utes and others, and it all could have been avoided by simply moving somewhere else.

Pride had a lot to do with it. Nate had been enormously fond of his uncle. The Utes had been trying to drive his uncle out for years, and when his uncle was killed, Nate had vowed nothing would ever make him leave. He pledged to make the cabin his home, and the world be hanged.

Looking back, maybe that wasn't the wisest decision he ever made. The site was too close to the foothills. Reaching the valley was easy from the plains below. Small wonder he had so many travelers intrude on his privacy. Small wonder the lives of his loved ones had been placed in peril time and again by every kind of cutthroat.

Nate was excited at the prospect of moving. A lot of work was entailed. Building a new cabin would take weeks, and he wondered if he could finish it before winter set in. If not, it would be better to wait until spring.

Then there was the challenge of convincing Zach and Shakespeare to move. His son was impossible to predict. As for McNair, Shakespeare had lived in that cabin of his for more years than Nate had been alive, and persuading him to give it up would take some doing. Nate wouldn't take "no" for an answer. He must convince them it was for their mutual good.

To think, a sanctuary no white or red man had ever visited except Shakespeare! A haven where they would be left in peace! No more fretting that a Blackfoot or Piegan or Blood war party would show up on his doorstep. No more worrying when his wife or daughter did something as simple as go fetch water.

Why hadn't he thought of this before? Nate shook his head in amazement at his stupidity. Sometimes the most obvious answers were those right in front of one's nose.

There would be drawbacks, of course. They would be farther from Bent's Fort, where he went to obtain things like bullets and salt and oil for their lamps. *Their lamps.* Profound sadness gripped Nate at the memory of all their destroyed possessions. Possessions that had taken years to acquire.

The worst loss for Nate were his books. Dozens of prized works, collected at considerable cost. His treasures, as he liked to think of them.

Nate loved to read. Even as a boy, he liked nothing better than to curl up with a book and lose himself in its pages. His father used to say that he read too much and reading was a waste of time, but his mother always came to his defense. Reading, she said, was a flight of fancy for the mind, a way to forget one's cares and woes. She read a lot, herself.

Nate thought it important to instill a love of books in his children, so nearly every night when they were younger he had read to Zach and Evelyn. In the winter, in front of the hearth; in the summers, sometimes out under the leafy boughs of a forest patriarch.

Evelyn always had liked being read to more than Zach, and it was Evelyn, as young as she was, whose love for books rivaled Nate's own. Zach's disinterest had been a keen disappointment to Nate. He wanted his son to take after him, but it wasn't meant to be.

As far as authors went, Nate had his favorites. James Fenimore Cooper was one. He never tired of rereading the *Leatherstocking Tales*. Natty Bumppo had been an early hero. Then there was Irving. Nate always liked scary stories, and *The Legend of Sleepy Hollow* had given him some deliciously chilly moments.

Among the other books destroyed were *Don*

Juan by Byron and *Prometheus Unbound* by Shelley. *Frankenstein* by Mary Shelley. *Ivanhoe* and *Rob Roy* by Sir Walter Scott. *The Iliad* and *The Odyssey*. Dante. *The Rime of the Ancient Mariner* by Coleridge. Plus many more.

One of his recent additions had been a book by an up-and-coming writer by the name of Edgar Allan Poe. The story, called *A Narrative of Arthur Gordon Pym*, about a sea voyage and the discovery of a lost land, fascinated Nate no end. That Poe fellow showed promise.

Now they were all gone. All destroyed. Years of scrimping to afford them, all for naught. Years of searching for various volumes, wasted. Books were not easy to come by, and were not cheap. He had been so proud of his collection, his "library," and now it was no more.

Nate would start over. Once the cabin was built and his family was settled in their new home, he would come up with a way to replace his books. Somehow, he would get the money he needed and make a special trip to St. Louis to order them.

That reminded him. Judging by the people Nate had met back east, he had the impression most Easterners thought mountain men were brainless clods who spent their hours grunting and scratching and were barely able to form a coherent thought. Nothing could be further from the truth.

Nate wasn't the only mountaineer who liked to read. McNair, Bridger, Walker, Smith, they all liked a good book. In fact, reading was so popular with the early trappers that during the snowbound winter months, when they were cooped in their cabins or dugouts, they devoured every book they could get their hands on. The Rocky Mountain College, the trappers called it.

Nate wondered why those in the States took it for granted frontiersmen were ignorant louts. He had actually met people who were astonished he could read and write. Shakespeare was of the opinion that Easterners were snobs, that they naturally assumed anyone who wore animal skins must be more animal than human. Or, as Shakespeare phrased it, "buckskins means brainless."

Nate tended to agree. Folks back east always did judge others by the clothes they wore and how much money they had, rather than what they were really like. Among some social circles, anyone who didn't wear the height of fashion and drive around in the best of carriages was beneath contempt.

Nate had been a victim of that prejudice when he lived in New York City. At one time he had planned to marry the daughter of a well-to-do businessman, and some members of her family had looked down their noses at him because he did not meet their standards.

In the wilderness there were no "standards." In the natural order of the animal world, there was no prejudice or bigotry. Mountain lions did not look down on rabbits as inferior, merely as food. Buffalo did not regard elk as social outcasts because their antlers were different. Hawks did not despise sparrows because they were smaller.

Only humans disliked their own kind for reasons

of their own devising. Only humans hated others for no other reason than their skin was a different hue. Only humans had the arrogance to despise those with less money or smaller homes. Only humans loathed their own kind for loathing's sake.

Nate never had understood how people could be so hateful. He never in his life had hated someone because their skin was red or black or because they lived in a hovel and wore rags. He never regarded the Shoshones or any other tribe as somehow less than human, as many whites did.

To Nate, the wilderness was how things should be. Every creature accepted on its own terms. Every creature dealt with according to its nature. No rich and no poor. No rulers or ruled. No creature telling another how it should or should not live. No laws to live by except the one cardinal law for all creatures everywhere: Stay alive or die.

The law of fang and claw, Nate liked to call it. The only law that mattered, because it was the only law that was real. All the others, all those man-made laws that filled legal tome after legal tome, were of no consequence whatsoever in the natural world.

A grizzly did not care that some humans thought it wrong to kill. When it was hungry, it killed, and that was that. A raven did not care that there were laws against stealing. When it was so inclined, it raided the nests of other birds and stole their hatchlings.

Humans as a breed had plenty of failings, and among them was the belief that the world revolved around humankind. That everything someone did, everything someone thought, was somehow significant. That all creation held its collective breath waiting to see what humans would do next.

Other creatures did not share the delusion. A grizzly was not impressed by how rich a man was, or the expensive cut of his clothes. All that mattered to the grizzly was whether the man made a tasty meal. A mountain lion didn't care if a woman was a social light in her community. All that mattered to the cougar was whether it should stalk and devour her.

Nate liked the natural order of things. He liked treating all creatures as their natures deserved. The only thing that mattered most to him was whether a creature posed a threat, and if so, how to deal with that threat.

At the moment, the main threat was Rabid Wolf. Nate had given the Ute the slip, but that did not mean Rabid Wolf would give up and leave him and his family be. Rabid Wolf's hatred ran too deep.

It had surprised Nate to discover that the red man was as prone to misguided notions as the white man. Many Indians hated whites for no other reason than that they *were* white. It had surprised Nate even more to learn there were rich and poor Indians, and that Indians lived by a code of conduct every bit as restrictive as the laws and rules whites imposed on themselves.

Among some tribes, for instance, a man dared not rush off to hunt by himself when a buffalo herd was sighted near his village. He must wait and hunt with the rest of the men in a communal hunt or suffer the wrath of the warrior society responsible for keeping order. That wrath might take the form of having his lodge cut into pieces, or he might be shunned by his own people.

Women who were intimate with men from another tribe might have their noses cut open to mark them for life.

In almost every tribe, only a handful held power. Those who had counted the most coup or owned the most horses or had the most gray hairs were the elite of Indian society. Their councils guided everyone else, and dissent was discouraged.

Having lived in both worlds, Nate could safely say that white and red were a lot more alike than either was willing to admit. Those who believed the only good Indian was a dead Indian or the only good white man was a white man the worms were feeding on would never accept that white and red were merely two shades of color in the rainbow of life.

All this, and more, Nate reflected on during the long hours of the day and into the early evening. He made camp in a wide gully and soon had a fire going. After putting a pot of coffee on to boil, he took the bow and roved in search of supper. When several grouse fluttered into the air with a brisk beating of their wings, he quickly raised the bow and drew back the string, but they were out of sight before he could loose his shaft. Then something moved in the bushes. It was another grouse, roosting low to the ground. Why it did not take wing, he would never know. But he was glad for the sustenance.

Stars blossomed. Nate drew his Bowie and sliced off a thick piece of meat from the spit and hungrily took a bite. He chewed lustily, then washed it down with mouthfuls of piping-hot coffee.

Moments like these were all too rare. Nate leaned back on his saddle and sighed in contentment. He wished Winona were there to share it with him. They so seldom had time to themselves these days.

The next moment, the bay and the sorrel raised their heads and gazed intently into the night to the east. Their ears pricked, and the bay stamped a front hoof.

Instantly, Nate set down his tin cup and the meat and was up and out of the gully and into the dark. He went ten feet and squatted. Drawing both pistols, he waited for whatever was out there to betray its presence. He did not wait long. A twig cracked loudly, followed by the dull thud of hooves.

Someone was sneaking toward his camp on horseback.

The night was pitch black. There was no moon, and the starlight was not enough to alleviate the gloom. Nate strained his eyes until they were fit to bulge from their sockets, but he could not pinpoint the rider's position.

It had to be one of Rabid Wolf's band. Maybe a warrior sent on ahead to find him and report back to the rest. Nate fingered the hammers to his flintlocks, eager to show the hostiles they had made a grave lapse in judgment when they had the chance to flee and did not take it.

The hoofbeats stopped.

Nate thought he saw—something—fifty or sixty feet away. It was no more than a vague bulk. Large enough to be a horse and rider. But Nate could not distinguish between them, and he did not want to shoot the horse.

The dark form started toward the gully.

His every sinew as taut as piano wire, Nate sighted down a pistol, but he still couldn't separate the man from the animal. His palm grew sweaty, but he did not lower the pistol to wipe it. He must stay ready.

Suddenly, the horse whinnied. Part of the bulk detached itself from the rest and melted into the well of black. Nate realized the rider had dismounted and was now on foot. With bated breath, he listened for the pad of a stealthy footfall but heard nothing except the wind.

A hint of movement to the right brought Nate around in a flash, his finger curled around the trigger. He pivoted so fast, his left moccasin slipped on loose pebbles and they rattled like so many hard kernels of corn on a wood floor.

The warrior was bound to hear.

Sure enough, there was a sharp intake of breath, and out of the night rushed a figure wielding a thick club.

Chapter Nine

Nate's finger was tightening to apply the final pressure when the figure holding the club spread its arms wide and happily bawled in heartfelt glee.

"Grizzly Killer! Me find you!"

"Chases Rabbits?" Nate was stunned. He figured he was rid of the nuisance. "I almost shot you."

The young Crow clapped him on the arms. "Me come warn you! Me see Rabid Wolf's band!"

"I know about them," Nate said, but the other babbled on without listening.

"Them hunt you! So me follow them. Me think maybe run off horses. But horses run off on own," Chases Rabbits related excitedly. "Now me come find you. Rabid Wolf mad. Want you dead plenty much."

Nate supposed he should be touched that Chases Rabbits was concerned about him. But he said irritably, "You should be long gone by now. I can take care of myself. I was the one who ran off their mounts."

"That you?" Chases Rabbits laughed. "Me see them run after horses. Catch some plenty quick."

"They did?" Any hope Nate had of avoiding more bloodshed was dashed. They would be after him at first light.

"One horse not run far. Use him catch rest." Chases Rabbits glanced toward the gully. "Me smell smoke but not see fire. Come slow so you not shoot." His teeth flashed white in the night. "Me do good, Grizzly Killer?"

"You did good," Nate begrudgingly praised him, although it might have been better if the youth had kept on going.

"Me get horse," Chases Rabbits said, and ran to fetch his animal.

Nate made for his camp. This was not to his liking, not to his liking at all, but it would hurt the Crow's feeling if he told him to light a shuck. Squatting by the fire, he resumed his interrupted meal. The meat was still warm, the coffee wonderfully hot. Soon hooves clattered and his young ally descended, leading his horse.

"Food! Me hungry enough eat buffalo!" Chases Rabbits licked his lips in half-starved anticipation.

"Help yourself," Nate said.

Heedless of the flames, Chases Rabbits ripped a piece from the spit. He bounced the piece from hand to hand while blowing on it to cool it. "Smart place for fire, Grizzly Killer. Rabid Wolf not see."

"That's the general idea," Nate said. Already he missed the quiet.

Chases Rabbits tore at the meat like a famished coyote. He barely chewed, and gulped. Grinning, he wiped his mouth with the back of his hand. "Best meat ever." He looked at the bow slung over Nate's shoulder. "Where you get that?"

Briefly, Nate told him. "They'll look for tracks in the morning and figure out I was to blame. Rabid Wolf will want my hide worse than ever. He'll trail me clear to the Pacific Ocean if he has to."

"That big water far west, yes?" Chases Rabbits asked.

"Yes," Nate confirmed.

"Hankton say more water than all rivers in mountains. Fish big like buffalo. Some many teeth. Some many arms. Some blow water out head." Chases Rabbits stopped. "That be true?"

"The ones with the teeth are called sharks. The ones with the arms are octopuses, and they're not fish. They look more like spiders with pumpkins for heads. Whales aren't fish, either. They're the ones that blow geysers out of their spouts."

"Me like see big water before die," Chases Rabbits said dreamily. "Me like see many arms. And whales, you say? So much me not see yet, so much me not know."

"There's a lot more to the world than the Rockies," Nate said to hold up his end of the conversation. He liked to read about foreign lands and foreign climes, but he had no hankering to see them. The mountains suited him just fine.

"People like us there?"

"Those who live in other lands have their own customs and wear different clothes than we do, but when you strip away the customs and the clothes, they are the same as us, yes."

"Have people like Rabid Wolf?"

Nate thought of Attila the Hun and Genghis Khan and Nero. "There have always been men like him, and I reckon there always will be."

"No place where people all good? Where no one try hurt others?"

"Not that I know of, no," Nate said. "Whites believe that when they die, they go to a place like that. They call it heaven."

"Me like go there," Chases Rabbits said in earnest.

Nate was observing a side to the younger man he never suspected existed. "In the morning I want you to head home. Swing wide to the south to avoid Rabid Wolf's bunch and you should be fine."

"You not want help?"

Choosing his words carefully, Nate said, "It's not that. I don't want you hurt, is all. Besides, Rabid Wolf is after me, not you."

"Friends no leave friends when trouble come," Chases Rabbits declared. "Me stay. Me fight."

There had to be a way Nate could talk him out of it, but try as he might, he couldn't think of a convincing argument. He had to settle for saying, "I want you to go and that's all there is to it. I won't have your death on my conscience."

A broad smile creased Chases Rabbits's countenance. "Grizzly Killer make happy. Grizzly Killer care."

Don't make more out of it than there is, Nate wanted to tell him but didn't.

"Me make mistake join Rabid Wolf," Chases Rabbits said. "Me wrong try kill you. Now me do right. Now me help you. Not go. Stay with you. You live, me live. You die me die."

Immensely flattered, Nate nonetheless insisted, "This is my fight. I'm asking you, man to man, to let me handle it."

Chases Rabbits fell quiet. He finished another piece of meat and wiped his greasy fingers on his legs. Then he said simply, "No."

Nate was on the verge of losing his temper. "Why not?"

"Rabid Wolf want me dead now. Him hate me like he hate you. My fight too."

The young Crow had a point. Nate could readily see Rabid Wolf wanting to slit Chases Rabbits's throat to show the other warriors what would happen to anyone who turned their back on him. In Rabid Wolf's eyes, Chases Rabbits was a traitor. Instead of killing a white, Chases Rabbits had befriended him. It would not do. "Leave him to me. I will take care of him for you."

"Me need help you," Chases Rabbits insisted, thumping his chest with his fist. "Me show me warrior."

Nate sighed, realizing he couldn't possibly persuade Chases Rabbits to change his mind now that the young Crow saw it as a matter of personal honor.

"So how we fight? What we do?"

"I need time to think," Nate said. Several ways to reduce the odds had occurred to him. He liked one more than the others in that if it was successful he would put an end to Rabid Wolf's entire band. So long as even one was alive, his family couldn't rest easy.

After his long day in the saddle, Nate was weary and looked forward to turning in, but for the next hour he was kept busy answering questions. Chases Rabbits was a boundless font of curiosity, and he was keenly interested in learning more about the white world. What did white people do? What were their lodges like? How did they make all the wondrous things they made, like guns and lanterns and fire sticks? Why did they wear such strange clothes? Why did they smell so strange?

That last one elicited a snort from Nate. Many Indians were hardly what he would call bouquets. Like most whites, a lot of Indians believed regular bathing was bad for the health. The widespread use of bear fat in dressing their hair added to their fragrance. So did the fact that some tribes mixed human or animal urine with the bear fat before applying it.

Nate finally demanded, "Didn't the white man who lived with your aunt tell you about white ways?"

"Some," Chases Rabbits said. "But me young.

Forget much." He showed his teeth. "Want learn more. Want savvy whites like savvy Crows."

"Good luck," Nate said. He had never been one to buttonhole others, whether a person or a tribe, because he had learned early in life that people were always more than the sum of their parts.

Chases Rabbits regarded him quizzically. "Why luck? Me learn all me need from you." He scrunched up his features in deep thought. "Tell me, Grizzly Killer. What you think whites do my people? Rub them out?"

"So that's what this was all about," Nate said. "You're trying to understand how whites think so you can stop them from doing to your tribe as they have done to so many others. Commendable, but it won't help."

"Why not?" Chases Rabbits asked.

"Two reasons. First, you can put yourself in white moccasins, but you can never view the world through their eyes because you're not white, just as they can never fully understand red ways because they are not red."

"Other reason?"

"There is nothing you can say or do to stop it. The whites will come, and they will come in numbers greater than there are blades of grass on the prairie. Tribes who resist will be wiped out or forced to live where the whites want them to live."

"What if tribe not resist?"

"There's no predicting."

"Me not want Crows die."

"I feel the same about the Shoshones." Nate

would not let them suffer the fate of so many Eastern tribes. They had taken him in, adopted him, treated him as one of their own. They deserved his help.

"That be sad day," Chases Rabbits said.

Nate did not need to ask what he meant. "My grandmother used to say, 'What will be, will be.' To her, there was no bucking fate. I've always felt we make our tomorrows by what we do today. There's always hope."

Chases Rabbits gazed skyward. "Future like big rock Black Beak push on us. Sometimes we get out of way, sometimes not."

Shortly thereafter, Nate put out the fire and crawled under his blanket. He half expected to spend a sleepless night tossing and turning, but within seconds of his cheek touching his saddle he was out to the world and slept soundly until the middle of the night, when a sound awakened him. He rose on his elbows. The first thing he did was check the horses. Both animals were dozing. Convinced it had been his imagination, he was about to lie back down when a god-awful noise filled the gully.

Chases Rabbits was snoring. Not light snores, either. It sounded like someone was strangling a goose.

Nate picked up a small stone and threw it into the air directly above the young Crow. Quickly lying back down, he pulled his blanket to his chin and heard his young friend gurgle and sit up.

"Grizzly Killer?"

Nate didn't answer. Grinning to himself, he closed his eyes and was soon dreaming of his trapping days when he rode the streams alone and did not hear another human voice for weeks on end.

The sun had yet to appear when they were on their horses and on the go. Nate had reheated what was left of the coffee, and between them they finished the little that was left of the grouse.

Chases Rabbits patted his belly and smiled. "Full belly good way start day."

Nate was fond of another good way, but she was miles distant. "Winona," he said softly to himself, and tapped his heels against the bay.

They were still days from the valley Shakespeare had told him about. Which was just as well. Nate had to shake Rabid Wolf off his trail once and for all before he got there. To that end, he scoured the surrounding terrain for the ideal spot, and close to midday, as they were struggling through a tangle of deadfalls, he glanced up the mountain and there was exactly what he needed.

"We climb," Nate said over his shoulder, and pointed.

"There?" Chases Rabbits was dubious. "Horses slip. Maybe break bones."

"It's a risk we have to take."

Talus slopes were always perilous. Covered with loose rocks and dirt, they were an earth slide waiting to happen. Nate normally gave them a wide berth, but not today. At the bottom, he drew rein.

"Me not like, Grizzly Killer," Chases Rabbits said.

"Rabid Wolf won't like it, either." The Ute and

his band would do as Nate now did, and start up exercising the utmost care.

"How you live so long, me never know," Chases Rabbits said.

The bay did not like the talus either. Purchase was tenuous. Stones continually slid out from under its hooves. They had not climbed twenty feet when the whole slope seemed to shift, and for a few harrowing moments Nate thought the bay would go down. But somehow the horse recovered, and when the talus stopped moving, it continued to climb.

Chases Rabbits climbed much more slowly. His body as rigid as a plank, he held the reins in tight fists, sweat glistening on his brow, the tip of his tongue jutting from his mouth. He did not speak except one time to loudly declare, "You crazy, Grizzly Killer!"

Another of Nate's friends, Ezriah Hampton, liked to say that "one fella's craziness is another fella's genius." Ezriah loved outlandish sayings like that. But in this instance it applied.

The better part of an hour was spent in reaching the crest, but Nate felt it was well worth the wear and tear on their nerves. For littering the top of the slope were dozens of boulders of various sizes. A few were as big as log cabins. A few came only as high as Nate's knees. Most were middling but would do just fine for what he had in mind. Climbing down, Nate sat on one to await the young Crow.

Chases Rabbits's buckskin shirt was soaked, he had perspired so much. When, at long last, his horse gained the crest, he sprang down, dropped to his hands and knees, and kissed the earth.

"It wasn't that bad," Nate said dryly.

"Not for crazy white man, no," Chases Rabbits said. "For me it worse ride ever."

Nate patted the boulder he was sitting on. "We made it. Now we'll see how Rabid Wolf does."

Chases Rabbits gazed down the slope. "You think maybe him fall? What good that do?"

"A lot if we help him." Nate grinned and winked. "Bring your animal." He wound through the boulders to an adjoining slope bare of talus and sprinkled with scrub trees. "We'll tie them here," he said. It was far enough that the hostiles would not spot them yet close enough that they could reach the horses quickly if they had to. Slinging the bow over his left shoulder, he turned.

"Now what?"

"We set out the tableware." Nate smiled at the young Crow's confusion and ushered him back to the spot where they had climbed the talus. Odds were the hostiles would climb it at the exact same point. If not, he had gone to all this trouble for nothing and put their lives in impending jeopardy.

"Where tableware?" Chases Rabbits asked uncertainly.

"Right here." Nate patted the boulder he had sat on. "Give me a hand." The boulder weighed more than a hundred pounds, but together they lifted it and moved it to the edge of the talus.

Chases Rabbits scratched his head. "What good this do?"

Nate pretended to give the boulder a shove with his foot, then gestured, imitating a boulder tumbling end over end to the bottom.

A fierce gleam came into Chases Rabbits's eyes and a wicked laugh tore from his throat. Smacking his leg, he hopped up and down. "Me like! Me like! You tricky, Grizzly Killer!"

"Don't stand there cackling like an idiot," Nate said. "We have a lot more to line up before they get here."

It was hard work. Some of the boulders weighed twice as much as the first. Each had to be balanced just right, with one end tilted out over the talus so all it would take was a shove to send it down the slope.

Nate left gaps between some of the boulders so they seemed more like a natural formation. Stepping back, he surveyed the rim and nodded. "That should do it."

Chases Rabbits mopped his sleeve across his forehead. "Me could drink whole river dry."

"I'll find you one later," Nate said. He sat on a boulder, shielded his eyes from the sun's glare, and scanned the timber.

"How long, you think?" Chases Rabbits wondered, sitting a few yards off.

"No telling. It could be five minutes, it could be five hours." Nate mopped his own brow.

"Me ask another question?"

"What's one more?" Nate responded. By his reckoning, it would make a nice, even five thousand.

"Why you marry Shoshone woman?"

"You ask the damnedest things, do you know that? Why do you think I married her? Because I love her."

"That not what I mean," Chases Rabbits said. "Why Shoshone? Why not Crow? Or Flathead?"

"The Shoshones were one of the first tribes I met," Nate related. "It could just as well have been your people or some other, I suppose."

"They give name Grizzly Killer?"

"No, that was a Cheyenne warrior who saw me kill a grizzly by accident." Little had Nate known it would be one of many. Shakespeare liked to joke that he had a knack for attracting the great bears, but Nate never found it amusing. Being charged by thousand-pound behemoths was not an experience most people cared to repeat.

"How kill bear by accident?" Chases Rabbits wanted to know.

"It's a long story," Nate hedged. He had gone to a river at dawn to splash water on his face and encountered the griz. Scared witless, he had backed into the river in the forlorn hope the monster would leave him alone. But it came after him. He had tried to run but slipped and fell. Drawing his knife, he struck blindly at the bear, and much to his amazement, the blade sank to the hilt in the bear's eye. It was a fluke. A one-in-a-million happenstance. And it saved his life.

"How many grizzlies you kill?"

"I stopped counting," Nate said. In those days, silvertips, as grizzlies were called, were as thick as fleas on a coon dog. They were everywhere on the plains and in the mountains, lords of all they surveyed, and they resented the white invasion of their domain. Early on, the mountaineers learned grizzlies were exceedingly hard to kill. Stories abounded of hunting parties putting ten, twelve, even fourteen balls into a griz and it wouldn't go down.

The early trappers shunned them. Nate tried to do the same, but every time he turned around, it seemed there was another griz, out to rip him apart. It got so, some of the trappers took to whispering behind his back. No one wanted to partner with him for fear he was jinxed.

Once Nate asked Shakespeare why he tangled with more bears than most ten trappers combined, and his friend's answer was instructive.

"I could say it's because you're green behind the ears. I could say it's because you like to explore places no one has been. I could say it might be something about your scent. Silvertips live by their nose, and maybe, to them, you smell different. I could say it's all of those things. But I won't."

"Then why?" Nate had persisted.

"Sometimes there are no answers. Sometimes things just *are*. Life isn't as predictable as some would like it to be. A lot of folks need to have everything fit into a little box in their heads. There *has* to be a reason for all that happens in their lives. To admit there isn't, to accept that some things just happen, is to admit life isn't as orderly as they want it to be, and they can't have that."

Nate wasn't sure he understood, and had said so.

"What does it matter *why* grizzlies can't let you alone? They *don't*, and that's all that counts."

It was one of the few times McNair hadn't resorted to a quote from Shakespeare to make a point.

Now, gazing down the mountain, Nate recalled the crucial kernel: *Some things just happen.* His father would have disagreed. His father was one of those who believed in an orderly creation controlled down to the smallest detail by its Creator. In his father's view, there were no such things as "accidents." Everything happened for a reason.

Two extremes. Was one more right than the other? Or did both contain a degree of truth?

Nate tended to take a middle road. He believed there was a higher power, but he took exception to some of the things that higher power let happen. How could the Almighty permit so much blood to be spilled? Why was hatred allowed to flourish? What purpose was served by one race exterminating another?

Nate never wanted to kill anyone or anything, yet time and again circumstances put him in a position where he must kill or be killed, and he very much liked being alive. Where was the rhyme or reason in that? There were days when Nate's only conclusion was that life was too ridiculous for words.

Suddenly, Chases Rabbits jumped to his feet and pointed. "Look there, Grizzly Killer! You see what me see?"

Seven ants were winding up the mountain. They

were a long ways off, but there was no doubt who they were.

"They'll be here in an hour," Nate predicted. Maybe a bit more. "We'd better lie low until then. If they spot us, they won't ride into our trap."

"Me can't wait!" Chases Rabbits declared. "Then it kill or be killed, eh?"

"Kill or be killed," Nate King echoed.

Chapter Ten

Nate King had to hand it to Rabid Wolf. The Ute had the instincts of his namesake. The war party came to the bottom and reined up. Rabid Wolf could see the tracks leading up the talus, but he did not start up it right away. Instead, he intently studied the slope and the boulders above, the very boulders Nate and Chases Rabbits were hiding behind.

Only Nate's right eye was showing, yet twice Rabid Wolf looked right at him. Or maybe Nate only thought he did. At that distance, he couldn't say what Rabid Wolf was staring at.

One of the other warriors, more impatient than the rest, goaded his mount forward so he could start up the slope, but a curt command from Rabid Wolf stopped him cold.

Plainly, the crafty Ute sensed it was a trap. Would he keep coming and count on his prowess to make it through? Or swing wide and scale the mountain from another direction?

Nate knew what Rabid Wolf was thinking. Avoiding the talus was the smart thing to do, but if Rabid Wolf was wrong and it wasn't a trap, the delay would put them another hour or more behind.

Chases Rabbits was nervously fidgeting, and kept sticking his head out and pulling it back again.

"Lie still!" Nate whispered.

"Why they not come?" the young Crow whispered back.

"Give them time."

"How you be calm?"

Nate wasn't. The wait was grating on him, too. Here was his chance to end it once and for all. *Do it!* he mentally screamed at the warriors below, but they sat waiting for Rabid Wolf to make up his mind.

Then came the moment of truth. Rabid Wolf twisted and said something to the others. Notching an arrow to his bow, he slapped his legs against his warhorse. The horse began climbing, picking its way with care as Nate's bay had done.

Rabid Wolf did not look at the talus. He locked his gaze on the boulders, alert for movement.

"Now?" Chases Rabbits whispered.

"Not yet," Nate said. This was the hard part. They had to lie there and let the war party get almost to the top before springing their surprise. His chin on his forearm, he tried to relax, but it was hopeless. He was too tense. It took every ounce of willpower he possessed not to start the boulders rolling sooner.

The minutes crawled by. Rabid Wolf was in no hurry. To the contrary, a turtle could climb the talus faster. Again and again, the Ute drew rein and looked expectantly at the boulders.

It occurred to Nate that Rabid Wolf was probably unaware he had lost his rifle. The Ute kept expecting him to pick them off from ambush.

Chases Rabbits glanced at Nate. "Now?"

"Not yet," Nate whispered.

The young Crow frowned.

By now five of the Utes were climbing the slope, spaced out at twenty-foot intervals. One of the horses abruptly slipped and teetered precariously, but the warrior managed to steady it.

Unexpectedly, Rabid Wolf shifted and shouted down to the two warriors who had not yet started up. They proceeded to ride north along the bottom of the talus, evidently intending to swing around it.

An unforeseen development, and one Nate didn't like: The pair could outflank them and cut them off from their horses. There would be no retreating if things went wrong. There was still time to slip quietly away, but then they couldn't spring their trap. Rabid Wolf would be as great a threat as ever.

Nate stayed where he was. His family's welfare was more important than his own. He would do whatever it took, even sacrifice himself if need be, to safeguard them.

Chases Rabbits looked at him but did not say anything. He did not have to.

"Not yet," Nate said.

The war party drew nearer. Rabid Wolf had his bow in both hands and was guiding his warhorse by leg pressure alone.

A little more, Nate thought. Another ten feet and they would be right where he wanted them.

Then another unforeseen development occurred. Rabid Wolf straightened and shouted, "Grizzly Killer! I know you are up here! I know you can hear me!"

Nate had forgotten the Ute spoke English.

"Show yourself, white dog, and let us end this! You cannot run from me forever! I will find you! I will kill you! Just as I will kill all whites!"

Rolling onto his back, Nate shifted so his feet were against the boulder.

"Why do you not answer me? Can it be you are afraid? Can it be your heart is filled with fear?"

Nate rose on his elbows high enough to see over the boulder.

"Did you think I would run away like a dog with its tail between its legs?" Rabid Wolf mocked him. "Did you think you could kill my friends and I would not avenge them?"

Chases Rabbits had done the same as Nate and was waiting for Nate's signal.

"I will count coup on you!" Rabid Wolf blustered. "I will count coup on many enemies and be a great man among my people! One day, maybe, I will lead them, and the land will run red with white blood!" He paused. "Do you hear me, Grizzly Killer? Are you trembling in fright?"

Nate would not let his anger get the better of him. He coiled, every muscle in his body primed.

"Why do you not answer?" Rabid Wolf taunted. "Are you that afraid? Show yourself, coward! Your gun against my bow!"

"Now, Grizzly Killer?" Chases Rabbits anxiously whispered.

Nate was watching Rabid Wolf. The Ute was scanning the boulders yet again. Their eyes met, and Rabid Wolf grinned.

"I see him, my brothers! The white dog is ours! We have him!" And Rabid Wolf tried to get his warhorse to climb faster.

"Now!" Nate said, and levered his legs outward. The boulder resisted, but only for a second. Then it was over the edge and hurtling down the talus, gaining speed rapidly. The sound it made was like that of a toboggan crunching through snow, only many times louder. Thick dust rose in its wake.

Yipping lustily, Chases Rabbits pushed his boulder and shifted to push another. "Die, Rabid Wolf! Die!"

Shock gripped the Ute. But to his credit, it was fleeting. Shouting a warning to his friends, Rabid Wolf reined to the right to avoid the boulder Nate had shoved. It missed his horse, but barely.

Undaunted, in swift succession Nate sent boulder after boulder over the edge. Chases Rabbits was doing the same. A horse nickered stridently and a warrior cried out, but Nate did not pause to look. Only when the last boulder was cascading down the slope did he rise up into a crouch. Even as he did, a boulder slammed into a horse, bowling it over. The warrior was sent tumbling.

So much dust choked the rest of the slope that Nate couldn't see any of the others. With one exception. Rabid Wolf was yelling at those below, urging them on.

Unslinging the bow, Nate nocked an arrow. The boulders had failed, but this wouldn't. As he drew the string to his cheek, however, the cloud of dust billowed between them, swallowing the Ute. Nate eased up on the string.

Another whinny rent the air. A warrior shrieked.

Leaping to his feet, Nate sidestepped to the left. All he needed was one clear try. But more and more dust was filling the air. Rabid Wolf could be anywhere. To almost have him, and then be foiled by a cloud of dust!

Over the racket made by the boulders and the yells and whinnies rose the clatter of hooves. Out of the dust loomed a rider, frantically trying to reach the top. Nate's hopes leaped and he spun, but it wasn't Rabid Wolf; it was another Ute who had somehow passed him and was almost to the crest. Nate loosed his shaft, but the Ute had seen him and wrenched aside. The arrow missed. Then the warrior was clear of the talus and rising to hurl a lance.

Nate had no boulders to duck behind. Nor could he retreat. He was too exposed. So he did the last thing the warrior expected. Nate threw himself at him, drawing his Bowie as he sprang.

The warrior let fly. The lance was a blur, cleaving the air like wooden lightning. Only the fact that the warrior's horse was skittishly prancing saved Nate's life. The lance passed over Nate's shoulder, and then he was close enough to sink the Bowie into the warrior's thigh.

Howling in rage and pain, the Ute drew his own knife and launched himself at Nate. Nate was bigger, but the impact bowled him over. He seized the Ute's knife arm as they fell. Locked together, they rolled side to side, each seeking to gain an advantage.

Nate heard Chases Rabbits yell something. Suddenly, the ground seemed to give way. The Ute looked up in surprise. Belatedly, Nate divined what had happened. In their thrashing, they had rolled over the edge and were tumbling down the talus.

A jarring pain seared Nate's back and the two of them were flipped into the air. They lost their holds, and Nate found himself on his stomach, sliding facedown, the talus as slippery as glass. Caught in gravity's inexorable grip, all he could do was thrust out his hands to try and stop his plunge. But all that accomplished was to have stones cut at his palms and fingers.

Nate was in the thick of the dust cloud. It got into his eyes, into his mouth. Each breath inhaled it deep into his lungs. Coughing and blinking, he saw a shape materialize in front of him. It was another warrior, on foot. Nate slammed into him like a battering ram and down they tumbled.

The warrior had a tomahawk and swung it at

Nate's head. Miraculously, Nate still had the Bowie, and he countered the swing, and another. Then the warrior struck a large rock, bounced to the left, and was engulfed by dust.

Nate remembered a friend of his who had been nearly torn to ribbons on talus. He was taking a terrible beating, but he could not gauge how severe it was until he reached the bottom. If he didn't smash into a boulder and split his skull before he got there.

Nate thought of his pistols and reached down to see if they were still wedged under his belt. Suddenly, the world exploded in bright fireflies and bolts of agony. He had collided with something. His senses reeling, barely conscious, he found that he had stopped. Dazedly, he roved a hand over the object he had collided with and felt a sweaty hide and hair.

Nate had struck a horse. The animal was just lying there on its side and trembling. He did not understand why until the dust began to thin. Both of its front legs were broken, with bone jutting out. It couldn't stand if it wanted. All it could do was lie there and quake.

Propping his left hand on the horse, Nate rose to his knees. His bow was gone. So were most of the arrows. He had one dust-caked flintlock, but the other was missing. He had also lost his tomahawk.

The crunch of sliding boulders had stopped. The rattling of talus was tapering off. Whinnies and groans replaced them.

Swatting at the dissipating dust, Nate winced. A

flap of skin over an inch long hung from his left palm by a shred. His middle finger had been cut deep.

"Grizzly Killer! You be all right?"

Nate shifted. Up on the rim, Chases Rabbits was flapping his arms like a goose trying to take flight. Nate smiled and nodded. His body was battered, but he was still breathing. He looked for Rabid Wolf and instead saw the warrior who had attacked him. One of the boulders had lodged fast midway down and the Ute had crashed into it headfirst. An eye was where the man's nose should be, and the mouth was a gaping scarlet font rimmed by shattered teeth. The warrior was dead.

Three horses were down. The other two were kicking and struggling to rise, but they, too, had broken legs.

"I'm sorry," Nate said softly, wishing there had been a better way. He scoured the talus for more fallen warriors and spied a pair of buckskin-clad legs sticking out from under a mound of rocks and dirt. Of the others, including Rabid Wolf, there was no sign.

Nate wondered where they had gotten to. Were they in the timber regrouping? Or had they had enough and were fleeing for home? He would worry about them later. The clearing dust revealed a more pressing problem. The horse that had stopped his plunge wasn't at the bottom of the talus. It was a little over halfway down.

"Damn." Nate could try to climb back to the top, but the talus had been so stirred up, it would be like trying to walk on shifting sand. His best bet was to slide to the bottom. One slip, though, and he would be cut up even worse than he was.

"Want me come help?" Chases Rabbits hollered.

"No!" Nate had to do it himself. He remembered how the sliding boulders reminded him of toboggans. He could use a toboggan of his own.

Nate stared at the horse he was leaning against. With two shattered legs, the animal was as good as dead. It might linger for days in the most excruciating agony, but its end was foreordained.

Nate drew his remaining flintlock. He blew on it to get rid of some of the dust, then carefully sidled close to the animal's head. The horse looked at him, its eyes wide.

"I'm so sorry." Nate cocked the pistol and pressed the muzzle to the animal's head. But he could not bring himself to shoot.

"What wrong?" Chases Rabbits yelled.

"Nothing," Nate said.

"What you doing?"

"What I have to." Nate stroked the trigger. He wouldn't have been surprised if the gun misfired, but it worked just fine.

Nate reloaded. It hurt his hand something awful, but he managed. The flintlock went under his belt. Cautiously crouching, he placed his right shoulder against the horse. Under normal circumstances, he couldn't possibly budge an animal that size. But all it took was one hard shove and the horse began to slide.

Nate jumped on top of it. Holding tight to the

mane, he rode the horse down as he might ride a toboggan. Only, this was a toboggan he couldn't steer no matter how hard he shifted his weight, and one that bounced and rippled under him as if the horse were still alive.

Nate grinned at his cleverness. There was a risk the horse might slide off the talus into the trees, but he would jump clear.

Then the animal lurched and canted and began to spin like a child's top. Everything was a blur. Nate couldn't be sure which way was up and which way was down. He thought he glimpsed a boulder. The horse jolted to a stop with a loud thud, and he was propelled into the air as if fired from a catapult. The sky and the talus changed places, and then he was in the talus and sliding faster and faster. His chin seared with pain and he tasted his blood.

A hard bump, and Nate experienced the sensation of flying. The world burst into a thousand shards and everything grew dark. He was not out long. He heard Chases Rabbits bawling his name and blinked up into the sun.

Lord, but he hurt! Nate licked his dusty lips and blinked his dusty eyelids and slowly propped himself on his elbows. He was flat on his back under the branches of a pine tree. His neck was wet, and in a panic he pressed a hand to his throat, thinking his jugular had been cut, but it was only blood dribbling from his pulped lower lip.

Nate moved his arms and his legs to test if they were broken. Every part of him, from his head to the tips of his toes, hurt. He started to ease onto his side, but a piercing protest from his ribs convinced him to lie still.

"Grizzly Killer! You alive?"

That struck Nate as the dumbest question he had ever been asked. If he were dead, how could he answer? He started to laugh, tried to stop, and couldn't. Maybe relief at being alive had something to do with it. He laughed until his ribs reminded him how severely they were bruised.

"Grizzly Killer! Grizzly Killer!"

Nate wished the young idiot would stop shouting. He would answer as soon as he caught his breath. Then a twig snapped and Nate realized Chases Rabbits was trying to warn him he was not alone.

Turning, Nate glimpsed a swarthy form with a lance. He rolled, and the lance bit into the earth where his chest had been. Pain washed over him, but he grit his teeth and stabbed for his flintlock. The warrior was unsheathing a knife.

Nate aimed and fired. The heavy ball caught the Ute in the sternum and smashed him halfway around. The bow fell from fingers gone limp.

His lips working but no sounds coming out, the warrior staggered, raised his arms to the heavens, and collapsed.

Where there was one there might be others. Nate propped his back against a trunk. Fingers flying, he reloaded. The woods were still, but stillness was often deceptive. He added the black powder and tamped down the ball.

"Grizzly Killer, me come down?" Chases Rabbits yelled.

"I'll come up!" Nate replied. Whether he could was debatable. Gathering his knees under him, he slowly straightened. Without the tree to lean on, he could not have done it.

Nate moved stiff-legged to the lance. With it for a crutch, he hobbled out of the pines. His right hip was terribly sore and his right ankle flared with pain if he put his full weight on it. He waved to Chases Rabbits and hiked north along the tree line, glad to be alive. Providence had smiled on him and he was thankful, but what Providence gave, Providence could take away, and there were still four warriors unaccounted for.

The talus seemed to stretch on forever. Nate had to stop twice to rest his right leg. High above, Chases Rabbits moved when he moved, halted when he halted. Nate hated to admit it, but he was growing fond of the silly chatterbox.

The absence of the pair of Utes who had gone north earlier puzzled him. Nate reasoned that they had heard the shots and the shrieks and come back to help. Yet if that was the case, where were they? He should have encountered them by now.

The talus ended. A steep slope sparse with vegetation rose before him. And there, high up, were the horses, where he had left them. He began climbing, but it was soon apparent his leg was not up to it. He stopped to let the pain subside and heard hoofbeats.

Chases Rabbits was bringing the bay and the sorrel down to him.

At that moment, the young Crow went from being an idiot to something more. Nate waited, his hand on his pistol, his eyes on the greenery. Rabid Wolf was out there somewhere, and Nate would wager every dollar he owned that the bigot was more determined than ever to turn him into maggot bait.

"Me see you hurt," Chases Rabbits said as he reined to a stop. "Me want help, but nothing me could do."

"No need to apologize," Nate said. He handed the lance up, then stepped to the bay and swung into the saddle. It was a mistake. Pure agony coursed through him.

"Maybe we camp here," Chases Rabbits suggested. "Grizzly Killer need rest."

"We're not wasting daylight," Nate said. It hurt to ride, but not nearly as much as it did to walk, and soon the talus slope was lost to view.

Chases Rabbits asked the question uppermost on Nate's mind. "Where Rabid Wolf be?"

"Your guess is as good as mine. When did you see him last?"

"When you fall down mountain. Rabid Wolf try shoot you with arrow. Me push boulder at him."

"You saved my life? I'm in your debt," Nate said, and meant it.

"Me not want Grizzly Killer die."

"You and me, both," Nate said with a grin, and nearly groaned aloud when his lower lip throbbed in torment.

"We find you water quick," Chases Rabbits suggested.

"That, or a bottle of brandy."

"What that be?"

"I'll share a glass with you someday." Nate paused. "I was fixing to give you a kick in the pants and send you back to your people, but you can tag along if you want."

Chases Rabbits had been riding a few yards behind, but now he brought his horse up next to the bay. "We friends, Grizzly Killer?"

"We're friends," Nate said. Further proof, not that any was needed, that life was a study in chaos. A few days ago, they had been trying to kill each other. Now here they were, riding side by side and offering invisible hands to each other.

Chases Rabbits looked fit to bust with happiness. "Me glad be your friend. Maybe one winter be more."

"What more is there?" Nate asked.

"Grizzly Killer forget pretty daughter? Me not forget her. She make good wife, me think."

"From friends to son-in-law in two shakes of a fawn's tail," Nate muttered. "Don't push your luck."

"Sorry?"

Nate mentally counted to ten before he said, "Forget about my daughter. She won't be ready to marry for years yet. Find a Crow woman who strikes your fancy."

"How many years?" Chases Rabbits asked.

"Ten or twelve, at least." Nate recollected reading about a duke or an earl back in olden times who made his daughter wear a metal chastity belt and locked her away in a room in their castle until he considered her old enough to wed. At the time, he thought her father had been too protective. Now he was sorry chastity belts had gone out of fashion.

"Maybe me wait."

Nate smothered a snicker. The odds of a healthy young warrior restraining his natural urges for that long were about the same as the world coming to an end. He had nothing to worry about.

"Grizzly Killer see," Chases Rabbits declared. "Me be best friend him ever have."

"I'd settle for a friend who knows when to talk and when to keep quiet," Nate hinted.

"What Grizzly Killer want talk about?"

Chapter Eleven

The deeper they penetrated into the mountains, the more wildlife they came across. Deer were abundant and showed little fear. Most of the time, the deer would stand and watch them instead of bounding off in fright. It told Nate that humans had rarely if ever been in that area. The two-legged locusts, as Rabid Wolf referred to them, always brought death and the stink of death, and it was not long before the wild things fled at the sight of a human.

Nate did not see many elk, but he found plenty of elk sign. Black bear sign, too, as well as that of coyotes, mountain lions, and more. It was paradise, unmarred by white man or red, and reminded him of how his valley had been twenty years ago.

Their journey had given Nate a chance to recover from his injuries. Though he still felt twinges of pain, the long days in the saddle weren't as agonizing as they'd been days before. He breathed deep of the rarefied air, and was invigorated. All three families could thrive here. There was more than enough game. And nowhere did he find any trace of Indians. Chases Rabbits mentioned that sometimes Crow hunters came this far on elk hunts. Nate found no evidence of Utes at all.

His excitement at the idea of moving grew. The thought of leaving the cabin he had called home for so many years plucked at his heartstrings, but there were things that had to be done whether a man wanted to do them or not. For his wife's and daughter's sake, if no other reason. For their safety and their happiness.

The only blemish in his newfound paradise was Chases Rabbits. He constantly badgered Nate with questions. Silly questions such as "Why white men have much hair on faces?" and "How can be no buffalo east of Muddy River when so many west of it?" The one that made Nate want to beat him with a branch, though, was "How many grandchildren Grizzly Killer want?"

Nate noticed that the young Crow was trying hard to speak proper English. In fact, Chases Rabbits tried hard to please him in all regards, which was annoying in and of itself. He had the impression Chases Rabbits was only doing it to impress him with what a wonderful son-in-law Chases Rabbits would make.

The youth could not seem to get it through his head that Evelyn was a touchy subject. Nate thought of her as his little girl, not as a young lady on the verge of maturity. He would just as soon she didn't marry until he had hair as white as Shakespeare's. To have Chases Rabbits keep bringing it up set his fatherly blood to simmering.

It was an inevitable fact of life that all girls became women, fell in love, and had little girls and boys of their own. But Nate could not help thinking that with maturity came a loss of something special, a certain indefinable innocence that could never be replaced. He tended to think of Evelyn, and Zach, too, as they were when they were young, and not as they were now. To him they would always be the little ones he had bounced on his knee in front of the fireplace, the little ones he had tucked in each night, the little ones whose hearts were golden and whose love was that rarest of treasures, love for love's sake.

Presently, Nate came to an unnamed stream, and beyond was a landmark McNair had mentioned, three snow-crowned peaks known as the Three Witches. The valley was not far now. He put everything from his mind and concentrated on finding it.

They followed the stream to where it forked and took the fork that wound northwest along a humpbacked ridge. Crossing to the other side, they paralleled the ridge for several miles to where part of it had buckled ages ago in a long-forgotten geologic upheaval, leaving a gap several hundred yards wide. The firs in the gap were so thick, hardly any sunlight penetrated to the forest floor.

"We go this way?" Chases Rabbits asked uneasily after Nate reined into the trees.

"What's wrong?"

"Me not like this place."

"Scared of the dark, are you?"

"No, me just not like. Bad medicine, me think."

In a quarter of a mile, the gap narrowed and they entered a canyon that meandered upward until they were thousands of feet higher. Ahead, the canyon seemed to end in open space. Nate slowed, figuring they would find a sheer bluff or cliff. But the canyon walls ended at the brink of a verdant slope that itself was part of a bowl-shaped valley hemmed by mountains.

And what a valley! Lush and green and bathed in rosy sunshine, a glittering emerald lake at its center, exactly as Shakespeare had described. On a peak to the northwest was the glacier. Flowing from it was a stream that fed the lake. A stream as clear and pure as any on God's green earth.

Jolted by amazement, Nate reined up. He had seen many beautiful spots in the mountains, but few that took his breath away like this. The trees were broad and tall, and had been old when the first white man set foot on the North American continent. Rich grass carpeted the bottom of the bowl, enough to feed a hundred horses for a hundred years. Snow crowned bordering peaks in ivory mantles.

"This special place," Chases Rabbits breathed in awe.

"There's no bad medicine here?" Nate asked, half in jest.

"You poke fun. This much good medicine. My people very much like."

Nate opened his mouth but closed it again. Time

enough to talk about that later. He gigged the bay down the slope.

Songbirds flitted among the trees. Squirrels scampered in playful abandon. A pair of ravens passed overhead, their wings beating rhythmically. Across the valley an eagle soared.

Everywhere Nate looked, there was Nature in all her wondrous glory. The valley had lain untouched for untold millennia. It was as the Rockies had been back at the dawn of time, as the whole world must have been before the advent of man.

The air was crisp. Sounds carried clear and far. The screech of the eagle, the squawk of a jay, the snort of a buck with antlers most hunters back in the States would drool over.

The valley was all Nate had hoped, and then some. He imagined three cabins ringing the lake, and walking along the shore hand in hand with Winona. Here they would be safe from the outside world. Here they need not worry about hostiles or cutthroats. Here was perfection, theirs for the taking.

"Grizzly Killer!" Chases Rabbits exclaimed. He pointed.

Nate had been so entranced by the scenic vista that he had not looked at the ground. Now he did, and a different sort of jolt speared through him, a jolt the likes of which only one creature on earth could cause. For there, clearly imprinted in the soil, were the tracks of a grizzly. A huge griz, by the size of them. The claw marks alone were nearly five inches long.

"We should go," Chases Rabbits said timidly.

"We just got here," Nate said. But the grizzly's presence added an unwanted element. The valley was the bear's home, and it might not take kindly to having its home violated.

It set Nate to thinking. Grizzlies were not nearly as numerous as they once had been along the Rockies' eastern fringe. But here, deeper in, they were bound to be as plentiful as everything else. For someone who drew the great bears to him like honey, it did not bode well.

The tracks were a few days old. The grizzly could be anywhere by now. Still, Nate rode with the pistol in his left hand. It wouldn't stop a griz. It wouldn't even slow one down. But it was all he had besides his Bowie.

Chases Rabbits had the lance, which he nervously hefted. "Me not want fight grizzly."

"And you think I do?" Nate would go to his grave happy if he never tangled with another silvertip. The thought of it caused his mouth to go dry. He looked down at his pistol and then, in one smooth motion, wedged it under his belt.

"Why you do that?" Chases Rabbits asked.

Nate did not answer. He brought the bay to a brisk walk, breathing deep of the dank scent of the woods. Pine needles covered the ground inches deep. Here and there shafts of sunlight pierced the forest like beams of celestial light from the Almighty.

The young Crow, whose eyesight was proving exceptionally keen, suddenly pointed again and blurted, "What that?"

In the shadows to the left was a white oval. Below it were what appeared to be uneven white lines. It did not look at all natural.

"Let's find out," Nate said, and reined toward it. He was almost on top of it when he recognized the white oval as the top of a human skull. An entire skeleton, clothed in tatters, lay partly against a tree. The white lines were the ribs, or what could be seen of them through what remained of the wearer's buckskin shirt.

"Him dead many winters," Chases Rabbits said.

Twenty or thirty years, by Nate's best reckoning. Swinging down, he squatted beside the deceased. Assessing the cause of death was easy. The skull had been cracked by a blunt blow.

"Him white or red?"

The tatters offered no clue. Then Nate saw a silver thread, and bending closer, discovered a silver chain with a locket attached. The clasp would not work, so he snapped the chain and held it in his palm. On the back of the locket was inscribed *To Micah, my one and only*. He pried at the seam with his thumbnail and the locket opened. Inside was a lock of blond hair. "It was a white man."

"Trapper?"

Nate surveyed the vicinity, but there was no trace of traps or packs or anything that would tell them what the man had been doing there. "I can't rightly say." Many of the bones had been gnawed on, and something, long ago, had cracked open the right thigh and eaten out all the marrow.

Nate was about to stand and climb back on the bay when a suggestion of color under the ribs prompted him to lean closer yet. A beetle came scuttling out of the rib cage, and he involuntarily recoiled.

Chases Rabbits laughed. "Bug scare Grizzly Killer!"

Nate bent down again. Tentatively extending his fingers between two ribs, he drew out a pencil-sized length of hardwood.

"What that?" Chases Rabbits inquired.

"Piece of an arrow," Nate revealed. With the barbed point still attached.

"Tell which tribe?"

"No," Nate admitted. The shaft bore faint painted symbols, red and yellow and maybe green, unlike any he had seen. The point, too, was not like any he ever came across. It was short, with sharp barbs that made it hard to pull out. A war arrow. Hunting arrows were fitted with longer tips rounded on their inner edges so hunters could extract them intact.

"Maybe Blackfoot," Chases Rabbits speculated. "Blackfoot kill everybody."

The Crows had long been at war with the Blackfoot Confederacy, so it was natural for Chases Rabbits to blame them, but Nate was certain they weren't the culprits. Micah had been killed by a tribe Nate was not familiar with. That alone was remarkable.

Nate had lived in the Rockies for decades. He had been to the Pacific Ocean. He had been to Santa Fe. At one time or another, he had met every tribe in the mountains. Or so he thought.

Placing the locket and the piece of arrow in his possibles bag, Nate stood and scanned the valley. Could it be, he mused, that the tribe lived there long ago? They weren't there now, or he would have come across some sign by now. He studied the mountains to the west. Beyond lay country that had never been fully explored. Perhaps the tribe was there, undetected all these years. "Have your people ever gone past those peaks?"

"Me think not," Chases Rabbits answered. "Why? Grizzly Killer not want go there?"

"One day maybe," Nate said. After he had built his new cabin and his family was settled in.

"Not go," Chases Rabbits urged. "Maybe not come back."

Nate suspected the Crow knew more than he was saying, but it was unimportant at the moment. Forking leather, he descended to the valley floor. Here he could better determine the valley's size. Seven miles in circumference was his estimate, with the valley floor running three miles from end to end. The glacial lake encompassed some ten acres.

The timbered slopes were unbroken except for the mouth of the canyon. Nate wondered if the canyon and the valley had been formed at the same time or whether the valley existed beforehand. If the latter, then the valley had been isolated from the outside world for untold ages, a pocket of ancient wilderness preserved in all its natural purity. Food for thought.

They came to the lake. Nate dismounted and walked to the water's edge. It was so clear he could see to the bottom. Sinking onto a knee, he dipped his right hand in and sipped. The water was cold and delicious, the best water he had ever tasted. Never in all his travels had he ever come across a lake like this.

Scores of tracks had been left by animals that came to drink. Deer, elk, black bear, a badger, opossums, raccoons, coyotes, foxes, bobcats. The prints of a large mountain lion were conspicuous by their size. But they did not interest Nate nearly as much as the set of tracks he came on a minute later. "I'll be damned," he said, and hunkered to examine them.

"What they be?" Chases Rabbits had not dismounted and was following a few yards behind.

"Wolverine tracks." A big one, too, and potential trouble for Nate and his loved ones. Wolverines rarely attacked humans, but their voracious appetites and fierce dispositions were not to be taken lightly.

Nate resumed walking. He had gone only a short way when he found what he had been looking for all along: more grizzly tracks. The prints here were clearer, the claws and the pads as distinct as if they had been made yesterday, when in fact they had been made more than a week before. He placed his foot next to one and whistled softly.

Chases Rabbits was similarly impressed. "Grizzly Killer sure want live here?"

"I can't think of anywhere I would like to live more," Nate replied.

"Valley plenty beautiful," Chases Rabbits conceded. "That right word, yes? Beautiful?"

"That's the right word, yes," Nate agreed. The valley exceeded all his expectations. It was everything he could ever want and so much more. He marked the course of the stream as it wound up the mountain to its source. The glacier was a gigantic white mass tinged with green that looked for all the world like the blocks of ice sold from ice wagons.

"Look there!"

High on an escarpment to the south, dark brown creatures with white rumps were crossing the sheer face. It did not seem possible that anything could find purchase on vertical rock walls, yet the creatures moved from foothold to foothold in apparent disregard of the dizzying heights below.

"Mountain sheep." Nate had not seen that many in a long time. Yet more evidence of the valley's unspoiled splendor.

The one animal Nate had not come across sign of, and which he would very much have liked to, was beaver. He was about to turn and climb back on the bay when another rare set of tracks gave him pause. He had to study them before he recognized them for what they were: mink prints. Like weasels and martins, minks were meat-eaters. They would kill anything they could catch, usually by biting it in the neck. Their hides, unlike beaver pelts, were greatly prized, and fetched a good price in St. Louis.

A grizzly. A wolverine. Minks. The valley was a treasure trove of wildlife the likes of which Nate had not witnessed since his early days in the mountains. Only then, standing there in the midst of so much bounty, did he fully appreciate the impact humankind had inflicted on the wild things along the Front Range, as some mountaineers were calling it. *This* was how it had been. *This* was how it should be. A deep sense of sadness gripped him.

It wasn't as if Nate had been blind to the changes. The beaver had been trapped and trapped until there were barely any left, but now that silk was the fashion of choice for fickle city and town dwellers, beaver were breeding in increased numbers and in a dozen years there would be almost as many as before.

Elk, once so common along the eastern range, now existed only in pockets at the highest elevations.

Wolves, once almost as numerous as coyotes, had been shot by whites every chance the whites got, and now only a few small packs roamed an area once home to dozens.

All this, and more, Nate had witnessed, and taken as the normal course of events. After all, no settler in his right mind wanted grizzlies and wolves nosing around his homestead. They were at best nuisances, at worst marauders, and Nate had not missed them one bit.

Until now. Strangely enough, Nate found himself

missing those days when the Rockies lived up to their reputation as a virtual Garden of Eden. He vividly remembered the thrill of those early days, a thrill long since gone.

Nate refused to blame himself for his part in the decimation. A man had to eat, didn't he? A man had to put food on the table for his family? He had done what he thought was right and he would not crucify himself over it. Hindsight always trumped foresight, because there was no predicting the future. A person made the best decisions they could based on events at the time, and if those decisions later turned out to be less-than-wise ones, well, that was the nature of the beast called life.

"Grizzly Killer!"

Something in the young warrior's tone made Nate whirl.

Up where the canyon merged into the valley, four riders had appeared. Even at that distance, Nate could tell the four were staring at him and Chases Rabbits. The riders were in shadow, but Nate did not need to see them clearly to know who they were. "Rabid Wolf."

"Him track us far. Must want you much dead." Chases Rabbits paused. "Sorry. Must want you very much dead."

"All this way," Nate echoed. He had constantly watched their back trail. Several times he had doubled back and waited for someone to come along. At night he always looked for campfires. And never, not once, had he seen anything to suggest Rabid Wolf was shadowing them.

"That only way out of valley," Chases Rabbits mentioned.

"Rabid Wolf doesn't know that," Nate said. For that matter, neither did they. There might be another way. But if it was, all Rabid Wolf had to do was wait up there for them to come to him and pick them off from ambush.

Even if they made it past him, Nate's dream of making the valley his family's new home had been dashed to bits on the hard rocks of Rabid Wolf's hatred. Because now Rabid Wolf knew of the valley. Now Rabid Wolf could come here anytime. Winona and Evelyn would be in perpetual peril.

Nate couldn't have that. After all the trouble he had gone to, after finding a haven like none other, he refused to let his chance to start anew be spoiled. There was a way to set things right. A simple, permanent solution. All he had to do was kill Rabid Wolf and the other three.

Chases Rabbits raised his lance to his shoulder. "How you want we do this?"

"I want you to wait in the woods to the west," Nate said as he climbed on the bay. "If I don't rejoin you by midnight, you're on your own. Slip away when you can, and tell my wife and my daughter how much I loved them."

"Wait." Chases Rabbits gazed toward the canyon. "You fight alone? What about me?"

"I'm the one Rabid Wolf wants most," Nate reminded him. "You said so yourself. So I'm the one who has it to do."

"Has what to do? Kill them? But that mine to do too, Grizzly Killer."

"We've been all through this." Nate was disinclined to go through it again. The young Crow would only argue his ears off. "Bring the sorrel and follow me," he directed, and rode toward the west end of the lake, away from the canyon and the four riders in the shadows.

Chases Rabbits was puzzled. "Why this way?"

"I have an idea," Nate said. He did not say what that idea was. When Chases Rabbits tried to catch up, he rode faster. Then, holding the reins in his left hand, he slid his right hand to the hilt of his Bowie and drew the knife without the young warrior noticing. Quickly, he cut half a dozen whangs from his sleeves. When he reached the trees, he slowed and called over his shoulder, "Keep an eye on them for me, will you? I'll explain in a minute."

Ten yards farther, Nate drew rein. He swiftly knotted the whangs together. Chases Rabbits had stopped and was doing as Nate had told him. Sliding off, Nate walked back, the coiled whangs close to his leg. "Are they still up there?"

"They not move. Why they not come after us?"

"Because Rabid Wolf is waiting for me to come to him." It was what Nate would do if he were in the Ute's moccasins.

"You mean us," Chases Rabbits amended.

"I mean me," Nate said, and leaped. His arms were around the younger man before Chases Rabbits had any inkling what was happening. Twisting,

175

Nate slammed him to the ground, not hard enough to hurt him but hard enough to knock the breath from his lungs and stun him for the few seconds it took for Nate to wrap the buckskin around his wrists and bind them.

"What you do?" Chases Rabbits found his voice. He struggled to rise, but Nate's knee was on his chest and Nate outweighed him by a good hundred pounds. "Stop, Grizzly Killer! Let me up!"

Nate had his Bowie out and was cutting off more whangs. Once they were knotted together, he applied them to the Crow's ankles, then smiled and stood back. "That should hold you long enough."

"For what?" Chases Rabbits demanded, and intuitively understood. "No! This not right! We friends, remember? Friends fight enemies together!"

"Friends do not let friends die for them. I told you it was mine to do." Nate took the lance and walked to the bay and mounted. He swore he could feel Chases Rabbits's eyes boring into his back as he rode past him.

"Please, Grizzly Killer!"

Nate set off across the valley.

"Not do this! It wrong!"

Nate was sorry he had hurt the younger man's feelings, but it couldn't be helped. The time had come to end it.

One way or the other.

Chapter Twelve

They weren't there, of course. They had watched him ride around the lake. They had sat their horses and stared as he crossed to the timber. Nate looked up as he entered the trees and Rabid Wolf and the three other hostiles were still there, still watching him. But when he came to a clearing a few minutes later and could see the mouth of the canyon, they were gone.

Firming his hold on the lance, Nate continued to climb. They would be waiting for him. They would pick their spots, and be ready. Four against one, and he with a pistol, his Bowie, and a weapon he had never used.

If things did not go as they should and Rabid Wolf came out on top, Nate hoped Chases Rabbits had the good sense to hide until the Utes left and then head for his village. Those whangs wouldn't hold him long. Maybe half an hour. By the time the young Crow crossed the valley, it would all be over.

Nate felt surprisingly calm. He must not let any of the Utes escape. They must not get word to their people about the valley. He had friends among the Utes, but as Rabid Wolf proved, he also had enemies. The fewer who knew of his new home, the safer his family would be.

Nate had never been much of a believer in omens, but it was troubling that his family had not even packed up to move and here he was, protecting the site he had chosen from invaders. It had better not be a harbinger of things to come.

The woods had gone quiet. Not a single bird warbled. Not a single squirrel chattered. The wild things, always sensitive to the presence of man, were hiding their own presence.

Nate hurt terribly. His pulped lower lip was the worst, although the gash in his shoulder protested every time he moved his arm. He could use a week to recuperate. Lie around the cabin while Winona nursed him with herbs and soup and her tender touches. Lord, how he missed her.

So many years over the dam, yet Nate cared for his wife as much as he had when they first fell in love. No, that wasn't entirely true. He cared for her *more*. Their love had deepened to a degree he never imagined possible. She was as much a part of him as his own skin. Or, more appropriately, his heart.

Funny, Nate thought, how life turned out. Never as a person thought it would. Never, even, as a person hoped it would. Life had a will of its own, and when its will and human will clashed, life always won out. One of the bitterest herbs to swallow was the discovery that in the grand ebb and flow of the river of life, human beings were no more than twigs, to be borne where the current carried them.

But that wasn't entirely true, either, Nate reflected. Human beings were not completely helpless. They need not always be victims of circumstance. They could carve a niche for themselves. They could live where they wanted, live how they wanted. He was living proof. He had left New York for the frontier and built a new life for himself. And he was happier by far than he had ever been back east.

Freedom has a lot to do with it. Nate cherished being truly free. Cherished being able to do as he pleased, when he pleased. West of the Mississippi, a man did not have someone looking over his shoulder telling him what he could and couldn't do. There were no laws to abide by other than the natural laws imposed by Nature. There were no rules to follow other than the personal code of each individual.

How sweet life was, Nate thought, when a person was genuinely free. When the only dictates they need follow were those spawned by their affection for those they loved. It was as things must have been back when humankind first appeared, before civilization and laws were invented, before humans imprisoned themselves in cages of their own devising.

What in God's name was he doing?

Nate drew rein, shocked at his lapse. Here he was, about to fight for his life against four foes who had no qualms about extinguishing his, and he was indulging in idle musings. He must empty his mind. He must concentrate on staying alive and nothing else. He must not let his attention wander even for an instant. Not if he wanted to hold Winona in his arms again.

Rising in the stirrups, Nate tried to see the canyon mouth, but the woods were too thick. He guessed he was a quarter of a mile below it. Close enough that he might encounter the hostiles soon.

The very next instant, an arrow streaked past Nate's ear and thudded into a tree. He had not seen the bowman, had not heard the *twang* of the string. Breaking into a gallop, he reined to the right while sliding onto the right side of the bay and hanging by his elbow and ankle, as Rabid Wolf had done that first day they fought. He traveled another sixty feet, then suddenly let go and dropped.

Rolling up into a crouch, Nate darted behind a pine as the bay went crashing off through the underbrush. With a little luck, the bowman would think he was still on it.

Something flashed through the vegetation a dozen yards to his left. Nate spun, raising the lance. He glimpsed buckskins and a swarthy visage, but the Ute was focused on the bay and did not spot him. Quickly, Nate ducked low and padded in pursuit.

The warrior was on foot, but he did not need a

horse. He was as fleet as a deer. Nate had to run all out to keep the Ute in sight. He saw him hop into the air, then abruptly stop. Nate stopped, too, aware that the crashing sound had ceased. The bay had come to a halt.

The warrior was intently scouring the undergrowth. He looked right. He looked left. He glanced into the trees. But the one thing he did not do was look behind him. He had taken it for granted that Nate was somewhere in front of him, a mistake Nate capitalized on.

Carefully placing one foot in front of the other, Nate drew steadily near. He was not Touch the Clouds. He could not throw a lance thirty feet and hit a target dead center ten times out of ten. He did not trust his aim at ten feet. He must be close, extremely close, much *too* close, if he was to lay the warrior low.

At any second, one of the other Utes might appear. At any moment, a shout might ring out and the bowman would spin and unleash a shaft before Nate could cock his arm. Or more than one shaft. Experienced warriors could let fly with six or seven arrows in under a minute.

Nate moved as stealthily as a panther. He made no noise whatsoever, and he was within fifteen feet of his quarry when the Ute did the unexpected.

The warrior turned around.

For a few seconds, both of them were frozen in surprise. Then the warrior whipped his bow up and pulled back the string, and Nate took a long step and let fly with the lance. Even as Nate released it, he dropped flat, and it was well he did, for the arrow cleaved the air above him.

The Ute twisted to one side, but he was not quite fast enough. He grunted as the lance sheared into his torso. Passing through his ribs, the tip burst out his back, low down, piercing his vitals and bringing him to his knees.

Drawing his pistol, Nate slowly stood. He started to thumb back the hammer, but the Ute was making no attempt to nock the bow.

Doubled over, scarlet oozing from his mouth, the warrior coughed and shook as if he were cold. Blinking in bewilderment, he gazed up at Nate and said a few words Nate did not understand.

How young he was, Nate thought, just like Chases Rabbits and Rabid Wolf. And now he would get no older. He would never marry, never sire children, never hold a grandchild in his arms. He had squandered his life for hate's sake. From the cradleboard to worm food in twenty years or less.

Gripping the lance, the Ute tried to pull it out. He lacked the strength. His stomach and thighs were red with blood, and a pool was forming around his knees.

A rustling noise behind him brought Nate around in a crouch. He scoured the shadows, but no one was there. When he turned back, the warrior was on his side, both legs quivering and his hands shaking. After a minute, the convulsions ended.

Tucking the flintlock under his belt, Nate gripped the end of the lance and tugged. It wouldn't budge. He tried again. He placed his left foot against the dead Ute's chest, bunched his shoulders, and put all his sinews and weight into it. Reluctantly but gradually, the lance slid out until, with a loud sucking sound, it was free.

Nate held it with the tip pointing at the ground so the blood dripped off. Then he hurriedly helped himself to the Ute's bow and arrows. He slung both over his right shoulder and, with the lance in hand, crept toward the canyon.

It wouldn't do to delude himself. He had slain one handily enough, but he must not become overconfident.

The silence grated on Nate's nerves. He paused often to listen, but he might as well be stalking ghosts.

A flicker of movement gave the next warrior away. It was high in a pine, and Nate might have dismissed it as a squirrel if he hadn't spotted a buckskin-clad arm amid the green boughs.

Dropping flat, Nate braced for the whish of an arrow or an outcry. There was neither. He studied the pine long and hard before he pinpointed the warrior, who was in a perfect position to spot anyone approaching the canyon. It was pure luck he hadn't seen Nate.

A thicket offered haven if only Nate could reach it. He began crawling, but slowly. Sharp movements might give him away. The lance and the bow and the quiver complicated things. He had to lift the lance an inch or so each time he moved forward so it would not drag on the ground, while the bow and the quiver kept sliding off his shoulder. He was barely a yard from the thicket when the warrior in the pine shifted and gazed in his general direction.

Nate pressed his chin to the soil but did not take his eyes off the Ute. Or was it a Ute? This one's buckskins were slightly different from the last. It was a Crow, Nate realized, a friend of Chases Rabbits's, no doubt.

Nate did not want to kill him, but what choice did he have? From the way the Crow was holding his bow, it was clear he would use it the instant he set eyes on him.

A bead of sweat trickled down Nate's back. He was too exposed, too vulnerable. But he resisted an impulse to rise and bolt for cover. He must wait. Stalking an enemy was no different from stalking an elk or a buffalo. Patience was paramount.

The Crow turned to the north, and Nate resumed crawling. He was relieved when he reached the thicket. But he was still not close enough to trust using the bow. He had to reduce the distance by half, if not more.

Reluctantly, Nate crawled toward the other end of the thicket. Threading through the thickly woven branches was a challenge. He held them as he went by so they wouldn't rustle.

Suddenly, a pair of legs materialized directly ahead. A warrior was slinking from north to south. Rabid Wolf himself, moving with the caution of his namesake. Were it not for the intervening thicket, Nate could have put an arrow into him.

Then again, were it not for the thicket, Rabid Wolf would have spotted him.

Nate had to lie there and do nothing as the Ute slunk out of sight. He waited a full minute to ensure Rabid Wolf was out of earshot before he inched forward. Intent on the spot where Rabid Wolf had disappeared, he did not glance at the pine until he was almost to the open.

The Crow wasn't there! Nate thought it must be a trick of the light and shadows, but no, after looking and looking, it was obvious the Crow had climbed down while his attention was elsewhere.

Nate was furious at himself. He couldn't keep making mistakes like this. One day a lapse like this would be the death of him.

Now Nate had no idea where any of his would-be killers were hiding. He snaked into knee-high grass. It was cover, but it rustled slightly no matter how slowly he moved, so he stopped. He would stay where he was and let the hostiles come to him.

The problem with that was Chases Rabbits. By now the boy was bound to have either chewed through the whangs or rubbed them on a rock or boulder to sever them, and was on his way up the mountain. Knowing Chases Rabbits, he would blunder right into a barbed shaft.

Nate rose to his knees. The other Crow had to be around there somewhere. He swiveled to the south, swiveled to the north. But the streaking shaft that sought his life came from the east. Had it not been for the lance at his side, he would have died then and there. But the arrow struck the lance and was deflected. It passed within a hair's width of Nate's eyes, so close that a feather brushed his eyelashes.

Casting the lance aside, Nate tucked at the waist and zigzagged toward a tree. He glanced back, trying to spot the Crow, and felt his left foot catch on something. It was an exposed root. He tried to keep his balance, but he was running too fast. Headlong, he pitched to the ground just as an arrow buzzed over him and struck the trunk with a loud *thwack*.

As Nate heaved erect, the quiver over his shoulder upended. Out spilled his shafts. He grabbed for them but caught only one, and then he was behind the tree and trying to still the pounding in his ears and the hammering of his heart. It had been close, so very close.

The Crow began shouting. Nate was not fluent in Crow, but he did not need to be. The warrior was shouting for Rabid Wolf and the other one to come on the run.

Nate had to get out of there. Backing away from the trunk, he notched the arrow to the bowstring. A twig crunched to his left and he spun and pulled the string to his cheek, and all the blood in his body turned to ice.

Not ten yards away was a grizzly. *The* grizzly. The one that had left the prints he saw earlier. Maybe it was not the largest Nate ever saw, but it was huge nonetheless, huge and broad with a massive head and the characteristic high hump on its front shoulders. And teeth! Lord, what teeth!

Teeth as long as knives, teeth that could shred a man to the bone with one bite, teeth the grizzly bared in an ominous growl.

Nate never told Winona, but he always suspected it would be a griz that did him in. He had tangled with so many since he came to the Rockies that eventually the odds would catch up with him. Sooner or later, he was bound to go up against one and the griz would come out on top. It was inevitable.

The bear raised its head and sniffed.

The Crow was still shouting. Nate heard the snap and crackle of undergrowth from two directions. Rabid Wolf and the other one were on their way. But he dared not move, dared not seek cover, not with the grizzly right there. It would be on him before he took three or four steps, and with only one arrow and one pistol and his Bowie to defend himself, he stood no chance, no chance at all.

Grunting, the grizzly shuffled closer.

Nate broke out in a cold sweat. After all he had gone through to find a new home for his family, to be slain by the one creature he had done his best to avoid in recent years seemed like the Almighty's notion of a warped joke. The only exception had been a bear known as Scar. It had killed dozens of people when he took up its trail and ended its savage spree. Otherwise, his attitude toward grizzlies could be summed up as live and let live.

Now this.

This griz was about to do what Nate had always known a bear would do one day. He sighted down the arrow at the grizzly's head, then lowered the bow. It was pointless. An arrow could no more penetrate all that thick bone than it could penetrate an anvil. He placed his hand on his pistol, but he did not draw it. Instead, he bowed his head and thought of Winona and Evelyn and Zach, and how deeply he loved them. "I'm sorry," he said softly.

Prepared for the worst, Nate looked up. For a few seconds, he doubted the evidence of his eyes. The grizzly was gone. Grizzlies could move silently when they wanted, but he was sure he would have heard *something*. It couldn't have gone far, but although he scanned the forest in all directions, it was nowhere to be seen.

"It can't be!" Nate blurted, and realized the Crow had stopped yelling and the woods were quiet again.

Nate ran. He had to put distance between himself and the hostiles. Again and again he glanced back, but much to his puzzlement no one was after him. A boulder loomed in his path and he skirted it, running half twisted so he could be sure he did not take an arrow in the back.

A shadow rippled across the boulder and a tremendous blow bowled Nate over. He thought the grizzly was to blame, that it had slammed him to the ground and was about to tear him to pieces. Then a dark visage filled his vision and a muscular hand holding a long-bladed knife swept at his throat. How he dodged he would never know, but he did, and locking his arm around the Ute's wrist, he heaved and flipped the warrior to one side but did not let go.

A cry was torn from the Ute's throat as his arm was nearly wrenched from its socket.

Nate rolled and lunged, pinning the warrior before he could rise while grabbing for his Bowie. The other's hand clamped onto his right wrist. Grappling, they rolled one way and then the other, each striving to sink his knife into the other. Nate winced when he slammed against a tree. He almost lost his grip. The razor tip of the Ute's knife was poised a whisker's length from his jugular.

Tensing, Nate smashed his forehead against the young Ute's nose. Cartilage crunched and blood spurted. He drew back his head and did it again, slamming his forehead against the Ute's mouth. More blood spurted, but the pain was not entirely all the Ute's. Nate's vision swam. Tearing loose, he leaped to his feet.

The Ute was much slower. Blood and bits of broken teeth were dribbling down his chin.

"Why couldn't you leave me alone?" Nate said, and drove his Bowie to the crossguard into the warrior's chest.

Stiffening, the Ute stumbled back a few tottering steps. His face was a ruin, his left side a crimson geyser. He was dead on his feet, but it took half a minute for his brain to shut down and his legs to crumple.

Nate's head was a drum. He could not think, it hurt so much. About to move on, he saw the Ute's bow lying near the boulder. Why the Ute had not used it, he would never know, unless the warrior had wanted the thrill of killing him up close.

Taking the bow and the Ute's arrows, Nate plunged into the verdant growth. Only two to go! But they would not throw themselves in front of his shafts or onto the Bowie. He must find them and slay them.

Several firs growing close together were enticing enough cover for Nate to move around behind them and lean against the largest. He must figure a way of luring his last two enemies to him. Shouting might do it, but it would tell them where he was. He was still debating what to do when an arrow flew out of the foliage and passed completely through the fir he was leaning against. He felt a sharp stab of pain and dropped to his knees. A glance revealed that the tip had sliced through his buckskin shirt and cut his flesh, but not deeply.

Another arrow whisked out of nowhere and stuck a fir at his elbow. Nate dropped onto his side and crawled to the left. He thought he was low enough to the ground that whoever was trying to kill him could not see him, but a third arrow disabused him of the notion by ripping into the dirt under his chin and raising puffs of dust.

Nate broke for cover. He was almost to a log when a shaft passed between his legs, narrowly missing his private parts. Throwing himself over it, he hugged the other side.

No more arrows were loosed in his direction, but Nate wasn't fooled. The archer was waiting for him to show himself. All he had to do was raise his head. But that worked both ways. Crabbing to the end of the log, Nate rolled onto his back and notched an arrow. He slid his possibles bag off, held it low against his hip, and took a few long, deep breaths.

Nate was ready. He must throw the parfleche as far as he could, and while it was in midair, he must sit up, raise the bow, and hope the hostile took the bait. And that was exactly what he did.

The Crow was in dense brush, only his head and shoulders showing, aiming an arrow at the possibles bag.

Nate's shaft streaked from the string. As if the world and everything in it were moving ten times slower than normal, he saw the shaft spin around and around yet unerringly straight and true. The Crow was ducking back down, but had not quite made it when the arrow ripped through his right eye socket.

Nate forgot himself. In his elation, he stood. He had done it! He stepped toward his possibles bag and his right leg seemed to catch on fire. But it was a trick his mind played on him. The leg was not really on fire—it burned from a gash in his thigh. As he stopped and gaped in mute incomprehension, another gash appeared. He had it, then, and he dropped the bow and palmed the Bowie while backpedaling, but Rabid Wolf was right there next to him, as grim as death, swinging a tomahawk like a madman.

Nate got the Bowie up, but Lord he was slow, as

sluggish as a turtle on a cold fall day. The tomahawk bit into him again and his left leg would not work. The next he knew, he was on his back and Rabid Wolf reared above him, the bloody tomahawk awash in sunlight.

It was about to happen and it was not a bear after all, just a young hothead who measured the worth of others by his hatred for them. Nate thrust the Bowie up to block the blow, but the tomahawk did not descend. It hung in the air as if frozen. The arm that held it was frozen, too, which was strange, so unbelievably strange, because the arm was no longer attached to Rabid Wolf's body.

Rabid Wolf screamed and tried to run, but a second swing of a huge paw broke half the bones in his body.

Nate lay there unable to move. The grizzly straddled him and sniffed, and he thought, *This is it, this is the real and final end. I am dead.* But then the grizzly did the most amazing thing: It turned and closed its iron jaws on Rabid Wolf's still-twitching form and carried the Ute off just like a dog carrying a bone. The vegetation closed around them, and Nate laughed, although it did not sound like a laugh. He said, quite idiotically, "I'll take that as a real omen."

Then Nate passed out.

Two days later, they left the valley. Chases Rabbits had bandaged Nate using strips cut from one of Nate's blankets. It took the entire blanket.

The young Crow insisted they stay longer so

Nate could build up his strength, but Nate yearned to see Winona and Evelyn and Zach. He would get plenty of rest and peace and quiet then. He thought that maybe, just maybe, he would get some on the trail, but he should have known better.

As they entered the canyon, Chases Rabbits grinned and said, "Me much happy you be better. It long ride to wooden lodge and me have plenty questions."

Nate King groaned.

Wayne D. Overholser
WILD HORSE RIVER

The Wild Horse River is the dividing line in San Marcos County, with the ranchers on one side and Banjo Mesa on the other. But the small ranchers and the Banjo Mesa residents got together to elect Jim Bruce as county sheriff, an act of defiance and a slap in the face to Holt Klein, owner of the huge K Cross ranch. When the owner of Gray's Crossing, a small ranch over the river, is murdered, Klein insists all the evidence points directly to the Banjo Mesa people. But Jim Bruce isn't convinced that everything is as neat as it seems. Could Klein be trying to set one side against the other? Asking questions like that will make the sheriff even less popular with Klein, and Holt Klein is a dangerous man to cross.

WILL COOK

UNTIL DAY BREAKS

North Texas, 1870. For three years a delicate peace has existed between the U.S. Army and the Comanche, led by Quanah Parker. The architect of this peace, General Tracy Cameron, has given an impassioned speech in Washington to plead for continued peace with the Plains Indians. His aide, Second Lieutenant Jim Gary, has been assigned to persuade General William T. Sherman that his plan for a military attack on the Comanche would be a deadly error. Meanwhile, Quanah Parker is organizing the Kiowa and Cheyenne to join him in an effort to drive the white buffalo hunters from the plains. As each side forms battle plans, a spark is all that is needed to ignite the frontier into total war!

Dorchester Publishing Co., Inc.
P.O. Box 6640
Wayne, PA 19087-8640

_____5369-1
$4.99 US/$6.99 CAN

WALT COBURN

BORDER WOLVES

This exciting volume collects three of Walt Coburn's finest short novels, two of which have been made into classic Western movies. "Rusty Rides Alone," a thrilling tale of a brutal range war, became the film of the same name, starring Tim McCoy. "The Block K Rides Tonight" is the story of Cole Griffin, who returns to Montana intent on finding the man who hanged his father years before. This story was filmed as *The Return of Wild Bill*, starring Bill Elliott. And "Border Wolves" draws on Coburn's own experiences as part of Pancho Villa's so-called "Gringo Battalion." Coburn paints the West not as it existed in legend or imagination, but as it really was.

TOM PICCIRILLI
Coffin Blues

Priest McClaren wants to put his past behind him. It's a past filled with loss, murder...and revenge. Now all Priest wants is to own a carpentry shop and earn a quiet living building coffins. But it looks like peace and quiet just aren't in Priest's future. His ex-lover has pleaded with him to carry ransom money into hostile territory in Mexico, to rescue her new husband. It's a mission he can't refuse, but it could also easily get him killed. Especially when he runs afoul of Don Braulio, a bandit with a great fondness for knives....

WINTER KILL
COTTON SMITH

Rustling is an ugly business. Just the suspicion of it can get somebody hurt—or killed. And there's a whole lot of suspicion over on the Bar 6, the largest spread in the region. Old Titus Branson is missing a hundred head of Bar 6 cattle, and he's mighty sure of who did it: Bass Manko. Titus isn't about to sit still for something like that. He and his boys are dead set on seeing Manko swing from a rope. But Titus will have to face someone besides Manko first: Manko's best friend—Titus's own son!

Dorchester Publishing Co., Inc.
P.O. Box 6640 _____5259-8
Wayne, PA 19087-8640 $5.99 US/$7.99 CAN

A TRAIL TO WOUNDED KNEE

TIM CHAMPLIN

In 1876 tensions run high on the prairie, where settlers push ever westward into Indian territories. Lt. Thaddeus Coyle is supposed to help keep the peace. Little does he know the greatest threat is from his commanding officer. Driven to disobey a direct order, Coyle winds up court-martialed and abandoned by his family. A ruined man, he finds his only friend is Tom Merritt—also known as Swift Hawk—a Lakota caught between his heritage and the white man's world. But when Coyle gets a job as U.S. Special Indian Agent and is sent to Wounded Knee, he and Swift Hawk will find themselves on opposite sides of the law on a prairie ready to go up in flames at the slightest spark.

VOICES
IN THE HILL
STEVE FRAZEE

With his eye for historical detail and unique ability to see into the hearts of his characters, Steve Frazee captures the very essence of the American West. In these five stories, collected for the first time in paperback, Frazee draws on his own experiences to bring his writing to vivid life. The title story tells of Riordan Truro, an old man who's been working in the mines so long that he understands the story behind every shift, every groan in The Hill. His fellow miners think he's touched in the head, but only Riordan knows The Hill has an ominous warning for those who work in its depths. Will he be able to convince everyone to get out before it's too late?

Ken Hodgson
FOOL'S GOLD

Jake Crabtree has been searching for gold for years. But he's pretty lazy and his luck has never been good, so it's no surprise that his search hasn't turned up much. Until now. Coming out of winter hibernation—when he usually goes on one long drinking binge—Jake learns that his benefactor, Dr. McNair, is at death's door. The doc's last request is to be buried on the claim that he shares with Jake. It's when he's digging the doc's grave that Jake finally strikes a rich vein of gold. But Jake's about to find out that gold brings with it a lot more than wealth. It also brings a whole passel of trouble and a pack of back-stabbing varmints!